Uncomfortable Silence

Uncomfortable Silence

by O M James

Mirador Publishing
http://www.miradorpublishing.co.uk

Mirador Publishing
Mirador
Wearne Lane
Langport
Somerset
TA10 9HB

CHAPTER ONE

There needs to be a review of the judicial system and indeed most senior justices need to have their competency questioned, they appear to have lost their way in the fog of senile dementia descending on the courtrooms in which they preside.

Simon Sanders made this observation as he sat in the living room of the now empty but once bustling three bed roomed house he had once shared with his wife and two children. They had because of his indeterminate behaviour moved out of the family home and were now living at her mothers citing irreconcilable differences as the cause of marital breakdown.

There could be an argument that he had gotten married late in life, he was thirty years old, his wife Donna was five years his junior. They wed after a mere eight months together, not because they were in love, although this was a sentiment not yet shared, neither of them thought to use contraceptives so when she fell pregnant, Simon realised to do the decent thing and give his brood a name.

By all comparisons, Simon had led an unremarkable but eventful life, however it was not a life filled with wondrous and exciting happiness. His gregarious and often engrossing personality was seized upon by jealously and resentfulness. He had a quick wit and an ability to solve everyday conundrums with a degree of ease - viewed as arrogance, often interpreted as conceit, veiled with selfishness.

He was the third eldest of four siblings, three boys and a girl born to Robert and Bridget Sanders. They lived in a four bed roomed house a short distance from a newly constructed complex of multi-or single roomed flats that were built in the middle of a neighbourhood of small town houses. Two-up, two-down houses renowned for their overcrowding of large family's of perhaps ten or more

people. These were once the backbone of the community. A community that had grown over the generations from landed gentry, shipping merchants, linen merchants, fuel merchants of the coal, gas and peat variety and those in the horse trade. Subsequently the area was peppered with small holding yards and stables, coal storage bunkers and large warehouses.

Gradually these magnets moved from an urbanite setting to a more rural, pastoral locale, leaving the region to be inhabited by the employees of the many mills and factories, effectively becoming a working class neighbourhood, full of life and vigour.

Alfonse Street one of the main routes into the area had capillaries leading off in all directions; Rose Street, Marle Street, Serbia Street O'Donnelly Street, Coventree road, leeson Street, Globner road and the Downs road. A plethora of other streets branched off to make an area named locally as the Pound Lonely, so named by the rag'n bone men whose horse and carts were regular sights to be seen.

The flats were seen as required social housing, at a time of great deprivation in both living conditions and employment that had rapidly disappeared over the years, were labelled a new beginning for the residents of the area in the capital city of Belfast, on the northern half of the divided island of Ireland.

Robert Sanders, Simon's father, was employed as a construction worker and was part of a team who travelled up and down the country demolishing, clearing and ultimately building whatever and wherever his employers were contracted for. The pay was decent, however, it also necessitated Robert to be away from home for long periods, often leaving his discontented wife to raise four children and keep a home alone.

For her part, Bridget was an independent, attractive, resourceful woman, with a fiery temper that matched her

long shoulder length reddish ginger hair, her beauty likened to that of the mythical queen of Ireland Kathleen Ni Houllihan. She also enjoyed the occasional bottle of wine at weekends but because of all the time she spent alone this soon progressed to five or six per week. Instead of the usual bottle of Australian red Merlot or German white Riesling at meal times, it gradually became an assault on the senses. There were carafes of wine neatly and methodically hidden about the house, they were more often than not residual dust collectors and an ideal place for the smaller creatures in life to dwell, Spiders, cockroaches, household bugs.

Bridget cared for her elderly mother who although in her seventies was well aware of her daughter's problem and often commented to how she was living in denial by not admitting to being an alcoholic. An accusation she flatly refused to entertain claiming the wine curbed the loneliness. Simon's elder brothers, William (Billy) and David had left the family home at the earliest opportunity, both having graduated to university within a year of each other. In reality, they were just happy to get out of the home they described as a nuthouse.

Billy went on to study law and became a successful lawyer David however decided to drop out of societal life preferring to travel declaring he needed to find his true self. No one had heard from him in years and it was supposed he was still searching.

Simon now two years into his forties, had seen and experienced enough drama and gut wrenching emotive issues in his short time in existence to have lasted two long and laborious lifetimes, each spanning eight decades or more… His thoughts of which there were many carried a philosophical nuance as he often alluded; "while it is true human continuance is reliant on survival of the fittest, most will and many often do lead an existence actively pursuing a proper calling in life, but not all. Much like the man or

woman who, after spending scores of years in an uneventful and unproductive relationship either discovers after the death of one, a true purpose for being. An unfulfilled romance that could have spawned a life of contentment, indecisiveness laden with insurmountable regrets over acts of ones youth, indifference at school leading to a life trapped in a world full of human drones and total inadequacies".

These were the contradictions enveloping the thoughts of Simon as he mulled and whined incessantly at the myriad of missed opportunity in a life now filled with meaninglessness.

He watched the six o clock news bulletin on the flat screen television which stood alone on it's plinth in one corner, a small but adequate speaker was attached to the wall in another corner designed to give the effect of surround sound. However, this was a poor substitute to the real thing as two or more speakers are seemingly required to achieve such resonance. Ostensibly, the other speakers had been smashed to pieces during one of the many arguments, which had become a regular occurrence since the onslaught of Simon's intolerable outbursts.

The news bulletin was airing an in depth story covering a man who was allegedly suspected of the sexual abuse of a minor and who for legal reasons was to remain anonymous to protect the identity of his victim. The notion that a perpetrator of such a vile crime was afforded any protection was "repugnant and an absolute outrage" thought Simon as he listened intently to the reporter outline the charges in a detailed manner.

As the case was concluding more revelations began to emerge, at the start of the trial there was no indication of whether the victim was male or female, however, with certain restrictions removed it was revealed that the accuser

was a man who had been sexually abused as a young boy, the alleged offences occurred some ten years previously.

"Who was there to offer protection for that young man?" uttered Simon who by now was eating the dinner he had prepared earlier. As well as being a television critic, he was also an armchair philosopher who had an opinion on absolutely everything. He was often heard shouting and bawling at the television screen, more often than not when his mouth was full of food. This was another reason his long-suffering wife packed her bags. Parts of the wall behind the T.V had become encrusted with half chewed pieces of food that she flatly refused to clean. After years of wiping and clearing the remnants of pigswill from her furniture, she had had enough. Even the poor dog 'Lucky', named by Simon's eldest daughter Bridgeen was not spared. Simon had given it to her as one of her Christmas presents. Lucky a little black mongrel half breed between a Yorkshire terrier and a Jack Russell was spattered with peas and potatoes and now cowered under the only piece of furniture remaining in the room as his ranting and raving continued unabated; as there was no room at her mothers, his estranged wife informed him the dog stays with him.

His interest in this particular case was all consuming, he empathized with the individual who had been wronged, he also assumed that the system was about to inflict further offence on the young man who was brave enough to have uncovered and revealed to the authorities the actions of this deviant. However, as Simon was well aware the judicial system tends to treat miscreants of this nature with a degree of leniency; Judges always impose light sentences for this type of behaviour. His opinion was absolute as he mused "it maybe a case of non-awareness or bad advice being offered or just not enough research into the effects of abuse on an individual but Judge's always seem to get it wrong".

5

During the bulletin, it was revealed that the case was to run for two weeks maybe longer dependant on the defence who were expected to call a number of witnesses to refute the allegations of the plaintiff. This only served to fuel an emotional tirade of expletives aimed directly at the screen, on this occasion however it was a more passionate and intense outburst.

He could not understand or fathom how or why this criminal could deny the charges that were conveyed against him. Not only did he ferry away the youngster's innocence so nonchalantly, effectively robbing him of his childhood and imagination, where especially in the mind of a young pubescent boy anything was possible.... Saving the lives of others as 'fireman' who rushes to the scene of a major fire in a big red flashy fire engine with its horns hooting and its lights flashing.

Or as a 'policeman' protecting the community and the public at large from criminals and robbers who steal hard-earned cash and possessions from long suffering workers. Making the streets a safer place in his white car adorned with flashing blue lights and loud siren chasing the thieves who attempt to steal away the night. A 'Surgeon' performing life saving operations, even a 'veterinarian' caring for sick and lame animals. Perhaps maybe even a professional footballer; he was reportedly destined to be captain for the local youth soccer team. He did, stated the manager show great potential. However, so many opportunities all disappeared in an instant because of injury and personal tragedy.

The alleged abuser was also branding this young man a liar, calling him a fantasist who was making all of the allegations up in his twisted little mind. The labyrinthine nature of children's imagination was complex and laborious with intricacies leading in all directions, the exception being the showing of sexual tendencies and the performance of

sexual gratification at such a tender age was unnatural. Children of a certain age should not be exposed to material of an adult mature topic. Exposure to such is a natural phenomenon, it can only be described as scandalous, the denial of freedom of choice is unwelcome the individual has freedom of choice and is not coerced into actions or activities that can only be described as an abomination.

As the news ended, the reporter added as a footnote the case would be concluded at the earliest opportunity. After almost two weeks, the initial two weeks had been extended due to legal arguments; the prosecution had made their final submissions. Tomorrow the case for the defence would commence.

Simon now calmed, settled down for a night in front of the television, this was nothing new as every night he settled down in front of the television. Tonight was different however as there was soccer on, his national team 'Ireland' were playing a world cup qualifying match against Italy who were deemed favourites to win the encounter.

He had an interest in all sports, Boxing, Golf, Snooker, Darts anything that could be criticized from the armchair. However, his particular sport was soccer and he tended to get intensely emotional whenever the team he happened to following on the night lost a match; no one was safe from critical analysis. The linesmen who sprinted for ninety minutes up and down the 100 yards of the football field making crucial decisions, sometimes right sometimes wrong were, as far as he was concerned dumb asses.

The referees who controlled the ebb and flow of the game were incompetents who had no concept of how the game was played, even though most of them were ex players retired through injury or simply did not cut the green and deemed not good enough to play the beautiful game.

The harshest criticism was aimed at the commentators, the faceless voices who described the action as it happened. These self-styled opinionated experts had the power to embellish any game with wonderful repartee, describing the action as sublime. On the other hand, their droll mannerisms when the game was being played at an awful pace had the effect to ruin careers and condemn soccer clubs into the depths of the lower divisions, these people had a lot to answer for. However vociferous he was with his opinions he was not always such a curmudgeon, as he would often say to himself in an aside, almost as if he was addressing an audience.

CHAPTER TWO

Simon's school days and his attendance at such bastions of discipline and learning were irregular at best. His absenteeism was outrageous as he just could not be bothered attending. Holy Family Lodge, a fully comprehensive secondary school for boys was the place he was to spend his second stage of learning. While it was unknown for it's canon as a school of great thinkers it often managed to produce a genius or two every decade. It was renown more for its reputation for toughness and its ability to soften the more rebellious variety.

His mother sent him every morning; and often to his own detriment, was easily sidetracked. Often he would fall under the influence of undesirables and critics of education. Effectively those who tend to live of the backs of the people who pay taxes and who contribute even less to society; those who have little or no ambition and are content just to be a number. They were neither friends nor associates but peripheral figures that tended to fascinate Simon's ever-expanding curious mind.

While he did miss a lot of schooling, he was always confidant of his abilities. He was capable of absorbing information retaining it and recovering it at will. From a young age, his head was in some book or other, picture books with large print to complex novels with intricate plots. He had an interest in all genres of literature and was equipped with an acute ability to express himself.

He sat, against the wishes of school authorities who deemed him ill prepared with a less than 50% chance of success for 'A' levels in English, Geography and History... although he passed with flying colours he supposed them

irrelevant. The cynics were baying for blood; teachers cried
'foul!', 'fluke!'

Those same ones who advised nothing would become of
a layabout were fuming with a red mist descending upon
their guise. Green also enveloped the atmosphere as Mr
Envy quite often took a chair at the table. While this
achievement was nothing short of astounding it was even
more special, considered an achievement by, a so-called
part-time pupil who it was feeling quite superior and utterly
pleased with himself.

Interestingly it was in his second year of school that his
struggle with the hierarchy began. In the first year of his
supposed five-year tenure of secondary education, he
entered into a class with eighteen others with an overseer
who was to shepherd them through their first term. It was an
apprehensive time for all the pupils as they started on the
long and quite often arduous road to maturity. Not only was
there the sometimes-daunting prospect of new beginnings
and the cultivation of pastures new, there was fresh
seedlings to be carefully preened and groomed with a
delicacy but firmness of hand. Coupled with this was the
electrical charged energy of pubescent boys, so many
emotions, so many questions, very few answers.

John Dory was to be their guide through this tumultuous
year, a forty something average size man who taught
English literature and music. He had been at the school for
over twenty years, however, this was his first excursion as a
form teacher and he was more nervous than his charges.

Simon Sanders and the rest of his new classmates filed
into the room and standing at the head of the class just in
front of a large dark brown coloured mahogany desk with
an unusual sized blackboard behind was Mr Dory. The top
of the desk was stained with years of ink and coffee spills,
positioned at each corner stood materials found on the
average teacher's desk. On the left hand, side a few

innocuous containers, chalk, pens, drawing pins and elastic bands. On the right hand side opposite standing one on top of the other, two trays with the words 'in on top and out on the bottom, apparently for marked and unmarked assignments.

The perimeter of the blackboard had octave's in batches of five with intricately and meticulously drawn musical notes edging along so as to give the impression of a railway track with exclamation marks, colons, semi-colons and full stops marking the intervals. On a ledge, running parallel with the bottom of the board was a six-inch long piece of wood that had a shape resembling a brick. This was tapered with one inch pieces of cloth felt on one side and was used as a chalk duster for the blackboard.

Just below the musical oeuvre, written along the middle in 2 inch letters were the words, MR DORY MASTER OF CLASS 1D. "Take note hollered he, 'D' indicates D for Dory, it does not as many of the so-called comedians have expressed denote 'dunce' or 'dummies'. There are no such people in this class".

The atmosphere was jovial with laughter and chitchat echoing the air as the boys attempted to position themselves in the small but adequately sized chairs and desks.

"Silence", hollered Mr Dory in a firm and authoritative voice,

"come come now find your place and settle down you are no longer in primary school, the days of mollycoddling are over",

"Firstly" he continued, "there will be no talking in this classroom You will speak only when spoken to and when attempting to orate you shall raise your left hand and wait until I notion acceptance". He then gestured to reading the roll adding,

"when I call your name stand up away from your desks and pronounce yourself as present, in doing so I shall be

able to see you in the flesh and observe you as an individual, not just a girlie speaking name"; he concluded by declaring "there are no teachers at this school, only your Masters"!!

If this was intended to be intimidating, it certainly had the desired effect for most of the class. Although Simon Sanders just supposed him peculiar, a fish out of water with an unusual if expressionless appearance, He was not fooled by the acts of bravado, as he commented to one of the other boys who he had become friends with "this clown is too dumb to frighten me".

Stephen Unlike who along with Johnny Hardly had become friends with Simon had suggested that he had better watch his back, as Mr Dory did not look the type to be messed around with;

"What kind would that be snorted Simon Sanders, the type that walks around opening his fishy mouth, waving his fishy hands searching for completeness like a gold fish swimming in a glass bowl?",

"you had better watch your step", replied Johnny Hardly, "he'll hear you",

"Who fishy Doc, fish don't have ears he mockingly replied". The name had a certain resonance about it and when everyone else heard about it, they all thought how befitting it was for their new teacher.

Mr Dory or fishy doc as he was now called finished his rant regarding the rules and casually strolled around to the front of his desk to sit in an old dilapidated chair. To the left of the desk just behind the chair a small wicker basket that had seen better days, stood unashamedly alone, with pieces of the wick protruding from every angle; there were strange looking stains upon this little receptacle, students could only hazard a guess as to their nature.

Class 1D became even more aware of this bizarre looking man, his hair tightly slicked back from his forehead

with what appeared like a pound of axle grease; his mouth opening and closing in tandem with rubbing his hands together as if to generate heat while he walked. He wore a black mackintosh style coat that looked as if it had been painted and vacuumed onto his thinly built frame; it appeared as if it had never been washed. The beginnings of an unwashed shirt collar could be seen peeking out of the top of the coat with the smallest knuckle resembling the knot of a tie piece holding the picture together. He carried an unusual odour about him; not an unhygienic offensive bodily odour but more of a liquorice leathery twang with waxing nuances, evoking images of a cobblers shop with its shoe master dressed neatly in his suit and tie, with his full length black leather apron as he mended and buffed the numerous shoes.

As he sat on the chair, it creaked and moaned like tired bones and joints that had grew wearisome through years of misuse and neglect. He reached over purposely and with meaningful intent glided open the top drawer of the desk, from here, he lifted a long ten-inch piece of leather that was 3 inches in diameter, menacingly he slammed it onto the desk, the attention of the class was captured as silence descended from every corner.

No one in the room had ever seen such a frightening object and all wondered its purpose.

"Say hello to Mr Pacifier",

Mr Dory cued with a slippery grin, the salivary juices quivered at the thought of using this once again offensive and almost surely illegal weapon on the poor unsuspecting children. The strap had evolved from the ruler, which was used to restore order in primary school.

"If anyone dares to disobey or ignore instructions," he explained, "they will be summoned to appear before me; if appropriate, correction shall be administered, their mitts", his reference to hands, "should be placed one on top of the

other and they shall feel the power of Mr Pacifier", - he concluded with a wry grin "are we clear"? The class responded with a low and muffled yet audible "y e s s s i r r"...

Introductions over and after a few more rules had been outlined the bell sounded for break-time, however, quite a few of the first year pupils were unaware of the nature of the sounding of the alarm, as in primary school there was no bell they were just told it was break or lunch time.

"So what do we do for break?", Simon pondered.

He soon discovered that the school was not equipped with facilities to be availed of at break time. Although there was a canteen/dinner hall to be used only for, those pupils who qualified for school meals. Fortunately or unfortunately depending on how you look at it, as one of Simon's parents was employed he did not qualify for anything free. This meant he was given a small allowance each day to cover his expenses, which included bus fare to and from his place of learning. "Small and totally inadequate" mused Simon. Usually apart from his infrequently taken breakfast, he was always returning home from school with a large hunger.

He never felt the need to eat first thing in the morning and had to be forced by his mother before venturing into the cold light of day. Only on occasion would he have a tiny morsel with his juice at break time and have a chip butty at lunchtime. This consisted of a medium size roll of white bread with the white fleshy core removed with nimble but experienced fingers, leaving a round perfectly formed hollowed out shell of crusty bread. This gourmet delight was achieved manually and was usually replaced with long undercooked stripes of potato resembling French-fries; chips that were, for essential taste dripping with semi-congealed lard.

Another filling applied to this menu entailed cheese and onion, Smokey bacon or pickled onion flavoured potato crisps which were purchased in small bags, crushed by hand and inserted with similar agility; a wholly anti-nutritious schoolboy lunch. All of this produce was purchased from 'pan loaves' the local confectionary hall that had the nerve to call it self a delicatessen.

CHAPTER THREE

The new school term had now entered it's second month and the situation appeared normal. Simon and the rest of the class that had been designated as 1D, their form and the class teachers surname had their introductions with the rest of their so-called masters. Some of them were apparently ordinary preferring to get through the working day with minimum of fuss with hardly an error worth noting. Others however, seemed to relish the prospect of instilling the fear of god into their protégé…

One such fiend was Mr Chronicle who taught history; if anybody committed anything the master thought of as inappropriately wrong, he would usher them into the tiny storeroom on the pretence of obtaining a new textbook or fresh sticks of chalk; once there he used his fists as a matter of correction on the unsuspecting recipient. There was a strong aroma of alcohol emitting from his person the influence unmistakable.

There was the usual student who after a barrage of fists and head butts always threatened to bring their father to sort Mr Chronicle out for his inappropriate impulsiveness. Often when the parents did arrive at the school, like a schoolboy Mr Chronic as he was later to become, went out the back of the school with the father and sorted the mess out. More than once it was to the fathers rue, no one was sure if this was allowed or more importantly, if the principle or vice-principle were aware of these events however it did appear to be acceptable violence towards students.

Simon and the rest of his fellow students, by the third month of induction started to feel increasingly worried; the notion was apparent that most of the masters were sadists who enjoyed bulling their young charges. This was further

enforced when one pupil of class 1d, James Nohop, failed for whatever reason to submit his homework to fishy Doc. Mr Dory had set what he considered an easy task for the class to write in their own words a short essay about their feelings and experiences of their new school. When asked for his reason for non-compliance James shrugged his shoulders replying that he had forgotten - this was simply the wrong answer, his nonchalance seemed out of place and ill conceived. It was blatantly obvious even to the young inexperienced Simon that some reason, any reason was better than saying you had forgot, any excuse will do at least you are giving yourself some scope to explain your folly; he was either ignorant of what was happening around him or just a stupid little boy.

Everyone could see the changing expression on fishy Doc's face, his lips quivered as his face contorted and eyes narrowed, steam could be seen emerging from his ears, he arose from his desk and summoned James to approach. James slowly walked to the desk he looked around, smiled in the direction of the class, and foolishly clasped his hands together as if to imitate fishy Doc

. When master Dory again asked for his reason again he shrugged his shoulders and refused to speak. Fishy Doc could sense the blasphemous attitude emanating from this unfortunate boy and promptly instructed him to "unfold his arms chest height and place one hand on top of the other with the palms facing upward". James still unfazed obeyed the order all the while still smiling and stared into the unknown. Meanwhile the class barely breathing looked on intently at the unfolding events. Every so often, a voice could be heard from the corridor beyond the closed door as silence gripped the air.

Fishy Doc retrieved the offensive weapon from inside his chest coat pocket, where he now kept it, presumably for quick access, raised it above his head and prepared to strike.

17

The colour from James's face and most likely his whole body drained and he was now ashen. Fishy Doc struck in a downward motion, giving the impression of a logger chopping with a heavy blade, onto those unfortunate static hands stretched out in front of him. The crack of leather against skin and bone reverberated and echoed around the room as lightening thunders through the darkened clouds of a distant storm. The class sat in stunned silence as this draconian practice continued with the sustained assault on the person of James Nohop as a further three strikes were inflicted.

He limped back to his desk he folded his hands that by now were swollen and crimson, up under his armpits in a forlorn attempt to hide from the pain. All eyes were on him and all could see the red evaporate as the pale descended upon his once cheerful face, a single tear emerged slowly from it's duct and trickled down his cheek almost in an act of defiance. However, it was abundantly clear he was broken and his compliance became absolute. Fishy Doc who seemed undeterred by his act of barbarity, casually strolled to the blackboard chalk in hand and wrote along the top in large capital letters, LESSONS TO BE LEARNED!!. He had reached a conclusion that this class needed to break free from their childish ways; they would have to endure a rude awakening in their push toward adulthood and he was not going to shirk from his responsibilities.

There was a method in his supposed madness although at first, this was not apparent, but in writing those four words across the board, where they stayed for three months of the first term, he was in fact conditioning his charges into a way of thinking.

As the school day drew to a close, the students of class 1d began to filter from Holy Family in small groups of three or four, each discussing the day's events. There was a general consensus among the children, who were

undoubtedly traumatised on witnessing the brutality of such an erudite figure, that if he ever tried that with any of them they would tell their father or tell my da as most referred to their patriarch. Simon Sanders was most vocal in this regard, as he explained to Stephen Unlike.

"if that growler ever tried that with me, my da would come here and punch his lights out. Stephen and Johnny both agreed, however, all three acknowledged the prominence of their teacher and vowed never to get on the wrong side of him.

Simon was also aware that if anything did occur he could not call on his father on account of his absence from the family home through work. An absentee landlord his mother preferred to label her seldom seen husband. Before the three boys separated to go to their respective homes, Simon had arranged to visit Stephen in order to share a problem he was experiencing with his French homework. Johnny lived three miles from Simon while Stephen lived just a mile down the road. Johnny who was vociferous in his damnation of French claimed,

"it would the first subject he would be dropping from his non essential themes for life", adding, "he could not get his head around the parle vous French language and culture". This indication was sufficient for Simon to exclude him noting he would be hopeless in assisting him.

CHAPTER FOUR

Simon arrived home to be greeted by his mother who appeared to be heavily intoxicated, crying and hugging his younger sister; "Christ" he thought, "She has started early", walked straight past the two of them, and went to his room, not even bothering to ask what was for dinner. As he sought solitude in his room, his mother called to him pleading with him to come down, as she needed to speak with him,

"What now mother?" cried an increasingly pissed off son, he stomped and foamed at the bit, opening slowly his bedroom door its creaking hinges exposing his emergence onto the landing as he reluctantly made his way down the stairs.

"reminiscing over better days and lost opportunities are we, when life was so much sweeter before you met my father?, if you stopped listening to that incessantly slow and laborious music maybe you could get on with your life".

He was referring to how over the years her drinking progressively got worse and more debilitating. It was almost to a point where she sometimes forgot who or where she was even though she had never left the same spot on the sofa for years. Normality had turned to abnormality as morning noon and night she would sit in her dressing gown and drink herself oblivious. Simon Sanders was also acutely of his mothers past, having been told on many occasions of her time as a girl, a teenager, a young lady and ultimately a married woman. Through her ramblings he learned how she had met his father in one of the many dance halls and church fetes that were so prevalent in her home village some fifteen miles from her present location of Belfast. In the days before the sale and distribution of the

20

demon alcohol, " I never took a drink until I met your father", was her old war cry.

Bridget was the youngest of three sisters and was born and reared in the small village of Ballymac, a quaint little hamlet with an extremely close knit community. She grew up surrounded by a countryside of rolling grasslands, fields of tall Ash and Elm trees and etchings of bramble, thorn and berry bushes, this place was where she and her sisters would ramble innocently away from big city life. Bridget had what some if not all women desire, older sisters for counsel, in times of trouble someone close to confide in. As she slowly matured the three sisters would attend the same dances in the hope of attracting a possible husband and here is where she met her future. Robert it was stated had attended the same venue on the off chance and he too was to meet his destiny or as he called her in his poetic musings his country rose. After a brief courtship they married and settled down in her home village.

Three sons later they both thought their family was complete and they went about the serious business of child development and when after a number of years of parenthood had lapsed Robert found his work opportunities suffering the same fate. Without consultation he dragged his family into the big city claiming he had a better chance of gaining employment, Bridget meanwhile could do little but acquiesce to his reasoning, had she seen the future her reluctance may have been more forthright. As far as she was concerned Belfast was an alien concept, a place where she knew no one and no one knew her and although her sisters were only a car or bus ride away she never felt so alone. Gone was all she was used to, her mother and father, her friends but most importantly her two elder sisters whose counsel was a crucial element in her survival; the familiar surroundings once so prevalent had been replaced by grey and dull brown. It was as if she had been picked up like a

rag doll out of some little girl's playhouse and tossed into the back garden. Her introduction to alcohol came soon after and slowly but surely, like a whirlpool, began to spiral onto the road of no return. These were the silent musings uttered by Bridget in her alcoholic stupors, she cared little who heard them preferring to weep at her own inadequacies while slumped in a chair.

At the same time, she would put on the gramophone and continually play the only two single playing 45 vinyl records she had. Both were played religiously: One a slow and meaningful tune by an artist named 'Acker Bilk' entitled, 'Ariel'. It was a musical composition without lyrics, it's melodious rhythmic saxophone sounding air was when first listened to easy on the ear, however, after continued repetitiveness it become more of a requiem for a death march. 'Bridge over troubled water' the other sole possession was played with the same rigour. This lament about brokenhearted loneliness and despair was sung mournfully by 'Paul Simon and Art Garfunkle'. Better known as 'Simon and Garfunkle' an American folk music loving hippy sounding duo popular in the late 1960's, 1970's and early 1980,s.

His mother although very drunk was stunned by her sons unprovoked broadside. When he had time to think about it he became very ashamed of his behaviour, never before had he raised his voice or showed his emotions. It became all to apparent however, that his mothers actions were increasingly unacceptable and something needed to change.

"You wonder why I never have any of my friends over," he would snap. It was blatantly obvious he was embarrassed by her, a secret better kept between four walls.

The outburst seemed to have the effect of instant sobriety. She caught hold of herself fixed her hair, adjusted her clothing in such a manner as to suggest she had been

afflicted with minute particles of dust falling inclemently about her person. She reached for a paper tissue from a small cardboard box, one of many that were littered about the room and, with a touch of elegance , wiped the tears from just below her bloodshot eyes. She patted her bloated and by now purplish red coloured face, almost as if she was applying foundation to her features which were well sculpted and perfectly formed. In Simon's opinion, she did not require false colouring to enhance her beauty.

She informed her son that she received a letter from his father and while it was mostly private, it did contain some unsavoury news. Robert had written to update his wife on his work situation, which had become frantic with new and more contracts being acquired by the company who employed him. He would not be home as he normally did; usually four times a year. He had been notified and had signed up for a further six months to a year which meant he would only be able to make it twice this season, having already been home once.

He concluded his correspondence with his usual niceties and romantic doodling and added almost as a footnote that he had asked his brother Hugh whose own home was being extensively refurbished to move into his home in order to have a man around. "To help out and suchlike" pondered Bridget, "I have never required help before, what is your father thinking of", she gasped, She was thinking out loud and speaking to no one in particular even though her two youngest were in the same room. "While the repairs are being carried out?, it was as if he owed him a favour" thought Simon.

There was a possible explanation for her husband's sudden and peculiar concern, for although he remained unaware of the domestic situation at his home. Bridget's mother was in regular contact with Robert, not as one might think to keep tabs on him but as a matter of deep

apprehension regarding her daughters and grandchildren's well being. She had obviously informed him about his wife's secret drinking leaving an increasingly exasperated Bridget to muse, 'mother', contemptuously to herself.

The fear and anxiety felt by all in the household was understandable considering the only time she had met Hugh was at her wedding and that was on the off chance. He had been away in America at the time the invitations were issued and it had been assumed he would not be there. However, like a bad smell he managed to show up. The moment she did meet him there was an instant dislike, she could not put her finger on the reason, it was just women's intuitive knowledge. She barely knew him and her children had no inkling of his existence but like most women she eased her worries by deducing her initial assumption on the rationale how much unlike like his brother could he be.

Meanwhile Simon who had listened to his mothers rant intently suddenly realised a great burden had been raised from his underdeveloped and somewhat small shoulders. Although he felt the same trepidation and unease as his mother, he also grasped the fact that his days of heavy chores were coming to an end. His schooling would now become paramount and more importantly he would be afforded more free time after his long days of learning, free time saved for weekends only. He could go rummaging in the forest or maybe go swimming at the local pool and get more involved in the day-to-day activities the same as many of his friends, in effect do what boys do.

Another reason for his joyousness was the relief he swiftly felt at the prospect of not having to care for his sister who had a never-ending illness. However, at such a young age he had no concept as to the seriousness of her condition.

Roberta was five years old and had been sick from the day and hour she was born. This was not the child's fault, she never asked to be born, nonetheless she was born with a

deformed heart; in laymen's terms this was open to interpretation with many hypotheses as to the nature of her illness. To use the true medical term she had an affliction doctors termed blue baby syndrome, a condition where the troubled person has problems with lung and heart function and is constantly short of breath. Their lips have a deep blue coloured appearance and in some cases, their complexion has a tinge of crimson attached to it. Most afflicted have a 1/5 reduction in life expectancy.

"In the grand scheme of life, the knowledge of the general public is wholly unbelieving" accented Robert and Bridget as they tried to cope with the rumour machine as it trundled though their private life. There were many hackneyed ideas as to the causation of the child's problem, from the mother consuming large amounts of alcohol and smoking during pregnancy to the father being abusive while she carried his brood.

Research undertaking by doctors however, suggest a genealogy problem more likely on the father's side. Robert at 49 was the eldest in a large family of eleven brothers and three sisters, the youngest a brother named George, who was born twenty-seven years after his elder brother. He was described as mentally sub-normal, had the intelligence quotient of 24 with the mental age of a ten year old.

Studies have shown that children born to women later in life tend to have health and mental problems. This was identified as a possible reason in the case of Bridget, who after bearing three sons waited almost ten years before having a fourth baby at the age of 39. The most grotesque ordeal for any parent is to witness their child in pain and it was heart rending to see the extorted and mind numbingly empty expressions etched on the faces of these hapless and disgruntled people. However, like wounded soldiers they picked themselves up and carried on the battle. They were informed that their child's condition was incurable, however

an operation to repair a defective heart valve would increase her longevity and with regular maintenance, she could live a happy, normal life.

There was a consequence to this, however, which carried a double-edged effect. The operation was successful and after a number of years of carefully nurturing and protecting their child, she became almost normal. A lot of stress and strain was put on the marriage during this period and was most likely the reason Robert found work in faraway places. It was as if he was joining the French foreign legion to flee a past life or escaping from prison where he was serving a life sentence for committing an unspeakable act.

Bridget began to drink heavily to as she reasoned to ease her pain, this only had the effect of the burden being placed on the boys. The eldest were quite obliging and often found it an honour and a privilege to care for their angel and princess the two pet names they had bestowed on their little sister. For the first years of her young life, Billy and David showered her with love and affection and would often take her to the beach when the fun fare was in town. Simon to, however, he was more of a peripheral figure as it was supposed he could look out for himself; at ten years old this was a large assumption.

CHAPTER FIVE

On one occasion an aunt, a sister of their mother accompanied all four of them on a trip to Wilkes Land, a holiday camp some fifty miles from where they lived. It was situated on a five-acre plot of land and was enclosed with high fencing. On entering, you paid a fee at the door, which entitled you to try all the amusements for free.

There were roller blades, swimming in a large pool that was adorned with tunnel shaped slides, there were high middle and low diving boards at one end with a shallow pool at the opposite end. In one section stood a snooker and poolroom, in another a tennis court with a table tennis arena attached. Dodgems and Fairground rides including the big bopper, a frightfully scary roller coaster that had the effect of taking your breath away and forcing you to lose control of your bowels.

In all the excitement Simon Sanders was separated from the crowd, at some stage he had wandered off on his own and was so immersed with events surrounding him he didn't realise his predicament. After a forlorn search for his brothers he decided to make his own way home and walked towards the perimeter fence.. As he got there, he saw a railway track on the opposite side and he climbed over, almost immediately he was faced with a dilemma. As he looked left along the track, he saw the lines ran in a perpendicular mode into the horizon infinitely, just as a bricklayer laying a plumb on a newly constructed wall to keep it on the straight and narrow.

After a quick 'inney miney mo', a process were one when faced with difficult choices or a directional conundrum decides with a little mind game using mental conscience; a nursery rhyme is used as a method of

27

elimination in choosing the supposed correct route or correct item. It is quite surprising how sometimes often large and important decisions are settled using this non-descript method, his choice made he turned right and so began his odyssey.

Side of the tracks was covered with bramble and wild gorse, there were plants and bushes and fauna, sights he never before seen. There were uncomprehending sounds never before heard, echoing all around him, however more than likely these were from crickets and birds and other forms of wildlife. His fear soon subsided and he began to feel awe and wonderment at the scenes set before him. He observed the bumblebees busily buzzing around the plethora of flowers searching for the amber nectar. The Johnny long legged flies which filled him with an unspeakable horror swirling around tumultuously not knowing which way to turn. The unusually oversized dragon flies reminiscent of helicopters hovering as if suspended in mid air were floating everywhere he looked.

All quite unpleasant he thought as he sauntered along the long narrow tracks. His nervousness began to increase and his mind started to wander; innumerable thoughts exploded in his head and he could feel the electrical pulses surging erratically over his now flushed and weary head. His brain felt as if it was being kneaded by unseen and unwashed hands. How far do they go he wondered, they would probably meet when I get to the end and that should be the end of the line he reasoned. He must have been walking for hours and as the sun began to set, he noticed the track began to fade - thoughts of food and hunger overwhelmed his senses.

The trek continued on it's perpendicular trajectory into the horizon and he thought of walnuts, of cakes laced with cream and jam sprinkled with ground nuts. He suddenly blurted out a thought, which appeared, at his forehead, "it

may surprise you to learn but I will not take that walnut cake". This was probably in reference to his mother's baking, and his loathing of walnuts. Baking was a past time she pursued vigorously to curb the tediousness and solitude incurred after suppertime. Where the hustle and bustle of a busy and somewhat chaotic kitchen created an atmosphere of family. A place with Children and adults squabbling over myriad of topics and to do lists, had been replaced with realms of nothingness.

Now his mother sobbed quietly in recollection as she created masterpieces equivalent to that of the renaissance. Walnut fancies with a nuance of earthiness, suggesting a hint of the herb parsley, while not to everyone's taste it was palatable with a mug of freshly brewed tea. The aroma of chopped carrots tinged with a hint of coriander broiling in the steamer.

Intermingled with these culinary delights loitered grated orange zest coupled with the seeds of the vanilla pod. These were delicately scraped from the gently opened stem, which was sliced down the middle with delicacy and finesse. A real bonanza to the senses, the perfume enveloping the room swirled and teetered in the air before being inhaled through the nostrils, travelled upwards and surrounded the brain with a soft pair of svelte finger tips, expelling lethargy and unwanted thoughts. The bouquet not only wafted in the kitchen and throughout the house but drifted effortlessly around the milieu, lingering for all to wonder as to it's foundation.

This particularly pleasing pursuit was soon replaced with a more destructive pastime. Bridget's drinking resulted in a continuation of constant nostalgic mode, consequently this would lead to her almost self-destruction . Gone was her beauty, her face was craggy and cratered, claret blotches replaced rose tinted cheeks, her hair now tinged with streaks of white and grey displaying an unwashed appearance. The

clothes she wore resembled a bag lady living rough on the streets of some dingy far off capitol city in the arsehole of nowhere. In this woman's mind, there was no hope, no future, only despair.

Meanwhile Simon's daydreaming was cruelly interrupted by a large hairy fat bee, the kind that always appear from nowhere with seemingly evil intent. The sight made the hairs on his neck stand to attention and his skin tingle with uncertainly. But he soon realised that this minute creature was probably as lost as he was and posed little or no danger to him. It was just searching for it's own kind, however, as the tension in his flesh eased his understanding of nature took hold. He began to grasp the notion that it was elemental as far as these communities were concerned and his fear was unfounded. He became reassuringly settled realising that no harm would come him.

His adventure had come to an end as he stumbled into what seemed an old abandoned railway terminal. This assumption was probably based on the fact that the place was deserted with a desolate feeling oozing from every corner. The smell of diesel and petrol fumes hung heavy in the air, there was however a ray of light peeking from a small office window situated along the long narrow corridor. Simon by this time was tired, cold and hungry, hesitated, unsure of the unknown walked towards the door, which was slightly closed almost, ajar and gently pushed it open. Inside there appeared to be policemen sitting about aimlessly doing nothing, he entered and the two spun in their seats and faced the frightened boy. The men in an instant showed their alarm and with a semblance of concern guided him to a chair placed a blanket over his shoulders and gave him some light refreshments.

Billy and Freddie worked for the railway and they explained that the station was fully operational but only maintenance or service vehicles travelled that particular line

and that was once a month if they were lucky. Billy stood around 5'6 and appeared to be around forty years old the same age as Robert, Simon's father. He seemed a likable type and carried a large apparent painted grin on his face. His outward appearance seemed jovial with a real rough neck quality, his face weathered and scarred from years of riding the service modules.

He inquired of his presence in the area "what has you in this neck of the woods, we don't often get visitors here?". Before Simon Sanders could answer he chirped in with a wry grin "maybe you are looking to steal our jobs, "Or maybe he is looking to steal our money". interrupted Freddie who appeared to be in his sixties with his bright white hair and bushy moustache that seemed to be tapered and treated with all the care in the world, a mans pride and joy. He also had large tea bag type loops under his eyes, which were darkened and stretched with age. With supporting lines that ran from just below the eye up and around his deeply matted eyebrows.

They both had a distinctive laugh, which tended to erupt from the depths of their throats and bounce off all four walls resonating up and through the ceiling; real characters . Simon Sanders informed them of his predicament and of the day's events and of how he longed to be home. Without a second thought Billy put the now almost sleeping boy into his van and drove him the fifty miles home. His arrival was greeted with nothing more than an exclamation of "oh there you are, you finally showed your face". As he was used to this, most attention was normally focussed on his sister, he shrugged and quietly added I am off to bed, he bid his goodnights as was customary in the Sanders household and slinked off.

Climbing the stairs toward his room he could sense the hostility hovering in the atmosphere, however, he was totally unaware it was aimed at him. Although there was no

consternation shown at him, directly, privately there was turmoil occurring beneath him. His mother was furious with Billy and David for allowing their young sibling to wander off alone. "What were you thinking" she cried, "anything could have happened to him, he could have been picked up by strangers and god knows what could have befell him". For their part the two young men just looked at each other red faced, took the onslaught and apologised profusely.

The most likely reason for the vain acknowledgment of his absence was probably due to the fact that while he was gone Roberta had taken a turn for the worst. She had been having trouble all day with her breathing, her little heart was palpitating an alarmingly slow rate. This in turn forced Billy and David to abandon the fun fare and rush to the hospital. Once there treatment was quickly administered and her condition stabilized. As a precaution she was admitted for observation and if pertinent would be released the following day.

Understandably Simon's whereabouts became secondary, Roberta the only concern. He had become a non-entity, a non-descript in a characterless, featureless landscape whose purpose and imaginary existence had succumbed to the realities of the present. However unpleasant and unwelcome it may have appeared Simon had to bite and accept the situation for what it was, a small hiccup in a bigger picture.

A few days later and after quite a few bottles of red wine had been consumed by Bridget the episode of the fare had not escaped Simon. His mother wailed and sobbed in her usual drunken stupor, "how could you be so silly and inconsiderate?", she demanded of her son. "As if I have not enough to worry about", she bartered and badgered him as a foolish little boy to the point where he had to flee to his room in hysterics. Openly he resented the scolding, secretly

he welcomed the attention, it gave him a sense of belonging
- a yearning to be noticed.

CHAPTER SIX

The arrival of Hugh, at the Sanders household almost went unnoticed. The remaining members of the family were to busy squabbling, with mother and son yelling and bickering at each other over some trivial issue. His appearance was greeted with a softly spoken hello from Bridget, as she tried to retain her composure with a hint of articulated sophistication all the while fumbling with her attire. Her soft white hands moved regally toward her hair as she continually attempted to mould and shape it with some dignity.

They stood in the living room area of the house and spoke in what Simon could only describe as a muffled tone. Whether this was intentional or just a private conversation he could not discern, however, the old adage of 'children should be seen and not heard' would apply in this regard as it was plain they were having an adult discussion.

The young boy sat on the stairs leading to the upper floors of the house when his mother called for him to come down and introduce himself. This was a moment he dreaded the most, as he was uncomfortable in the company of strangers. He became agitated and anxious at the prospect of meeting what was in a certain respect his temporary father. Although he had in the not to distant past been in the company of the two railway workers Billy and Freddie who were undoubtedly strangers, he had through necessity entered their domain for assistance and solace. This situation was completely different however as an outsider had entered his realm, his comfort zone had been breached and he would have to adapt to the new dispensation.

Simon Sanders slowly descended the stairs and inched nervously toward the room in which his mother and soon to

be introduced Uncle were standing. He peered into the room and was greeted with an image straight from the pages of a 'Jonathan Swift' novel. There beside his mother stood what first impressions would describe as a vagrant, a hobo fresh off the carriage of a cargo train who was pleading for a bed for the night.

Hugh stood in the centre of the room his hair bedraggled and unwashed and in no particular style. More akin to one of his sister's old shabby dolls casually tossed into the corner as she became tired and weary of it; like most new things the novelty soon fades. His face appeared weathered and wind swept, he wore a tuft beard that was clumped with colours of ginger and white, intermingled with dark patches, which was presumably his natural colour. The clothes he wore had seen better days, dishevelled and dirty as if appearance to this nondescript was secondary. A beige dress jacket with stained lapels was draped over his thinly built frame, beneath this there was a white chewing gum coloured shirt with frills that hung from the front. His black denims and squelched brown boots that had not seen a lick of polish from the day and hour they were purchased completed the picture.

Over one shoulder hung a large and bulky hover sack presumably carrying his belongings, this to appeared worn and shaggy. He also carried a strange shaped case Simon Sanders was later to discover was for a banjo, a musical instrument similar to a guitar he apparently played. "Quite bizarre and strange", thought Simon, however this was how this misfit preferred to introduce himself.

He spoke with a strange accent as he gestured to Simon to come into the room. "How are you my boy?", he uttered, "I'm your father's brother Hugh and I will be staying for a while to help your mum out, it is pretty clear she needs a helping hand as she looks worn out". Simon Sanders was

puzzled at this remark it was almost as if he was implying that he was lazy and never pulled his weight.

"So tell me what your name is?", he inquired of the now disinterested Simon who by now sat on the edge of the sofa. The questions continued for what seemed like forever and as he withdrew after the niceties concluded he could not help having a real sense of foreboding about this peculiar looking man. The most disturbing element concerning his appearance was his eyes. Green in colour and wider apart than any he had ever seen, they appeared untrustworthy and glaring with knife like tendencies that made the hair on the back of his neck stand to attention.

He would be staying in the elder boys old room his mother informed him. Simon objected immediately by informing her of the locality to his room. "We don't know this man", he cried, "why can't he stay up in the attic. There is more than enough room to place a bed into it, it would not take long to make it liveable again". However, his mother was unwavering and insisted that he stays in the elder boy's room.

"It won't be for long", his mother said in a vain attempt to reassure her son, "your father should be home in a few months once his current contract is completed", at that the discussion came to a close.

The mood appeared jovial as one and all meandered about the large house, Simon was busily doing nothing in his room. His class was assigned the novel 'Shane' by the author 'Jack Schaefer', a story of age old hostilities in the wild west of America in the 1800's, where a young boy of impressionable age witnesses the evils of human character. This was sited on his bedside table opened with one of the pages marked with a dog-ear in order to remind him of his place. Also littered around the room were books of Latin and Greek. Virgil's the Aeneid and the Annals and Histories by the Roman historian Tacitus. Also included in the library

were the Odyssey and the Iliad, Untranslated Greek epics by Homer.

These belonged to Billy who had studied them while at university. Simon had removed them from his older brother's room in order to read, however his understanding of the tongue provided a barrier to elucidation. As he lazed idly he heard rufflings from the next room, the sound reminiscent of something being dragged across the floor. A sofa without wheels, a sack of coal too heavy for one person to lift laboriously pulled and shunted into it's bunker. He went to investigate and discovered Hugh moving his belongings into the sanctuary of the brother's room.

He watched as his uncle desecrated this haven with his presence,

"how long do you intend on being here he enquired?",

"not long son, just until your father returns",

Hugh replied in a matter of fact tone,

"Your mother is under pressure and requires assistance, I am not here taking anyone's place just providing a helping hand".

It seemed he was attempting to dismiss any bad feeling for his being there. This was further enhanced by the revelation that if he were at all interested he would teach him to play the banjo.

"no I am not I have no desire to play such instrument" snapped Simon.

"Okay I heard that" replied Hugh "but it is a lost opportunity to build on your abilities, citing a musical instrument as part of your expertise will go a long way when you are older".

Simon was adamant and he also resented the fact of his uncle referring to him as son.

Although it was a term of endearment where the user affectionately labels someone they care for or have concerns about. Simon's mind was full of mixed up thoughts and

ideas, he was of the opinion that Hugh was not only there as assistance to his mother he was also attempting to be a replacement for his father.

"Don't call me son and don't ever try to fill my fathers shoes" he quipped in the sternest voice he could muster. This took his uncle by surprise, surprise that such assertiveness came from so small a boy. Before he could gather a response Simon was back in his room slamming the door behind him.

He stood in the centre of the room huffing and puffing with excited rage, his face crimson, beads of sweat trickled down his forehead as a tempest of butterflies swirled in his knotted stomach. He wondered where he had got the strength for such an outburst. "That will teach him" he mused as he kicked off his shoes and lay down on the bed and fell into a restless sleep.

Simon missed his father and he was determined not to let this so-called uncle who was in fact a stranger who had shown little respect in his words and actions get to comfy with his surroundings. Seemingly it appeared he had beguiled his mother with his charm and wit, Simon seen this as arrogance not to be trusted.

Sometime later when it was dark he awoke to the sound of music filtering through the house; as he sat up he realised the sound was emanating from the next room. It was a familiar sound almost as if he had it heard before, similar to a guitar only it had a sharper twang. Hugh was playing his banjo with a great deal of gusto and ostensibly very loud. This intrigued Simon and he went to investigate; the brother's room was slightly bigger than his own but it now appeared more spacious giving it was devoid of human activity.

All of their belongings had been long since removed apart from a few tattered and torn wall posters that hung precariously from one of the walls that faced the window.

'Albert Einstein' and 'R.J Oppenheimmer' stared intently through the glass at the open sky. Two small beds ran in an east west fashion at opposite ends of the room, with a small apparently antique cabinet placed as a divider between them. The centre of the room was occupied with a circular remnant of carpet, which had an indeterminate design splashed across it, excess from a larger roll adorning the living quarters below. As he pushed open the door he saw his uncle sitting at the right side on edge of the bed plectrum in hand plucking the chords.

It was a repetitive air he played that seemed to gradually build and build before returning to the start. He sat in almost darkness with just a smidgin of light stuttering from the bedside cabinet lamp.

"Do you like the tune?" his uncle enquired. He paused from playing to inhale another draw from the cigarette that was smouldering on the edge of the antique.

"Yes" he replied excitedly entering the room unconcerned. "What was that you were playing, is it hard to do and can I have a try?"

"Patience my boy you have crawl before you walk" answered his uncle. He stood up and placed the instrument on the bed and walked to close the door, as he did Simon reached for the banjo.

In an instant Hugh was behind him uttering almost silently "wait and I will show you how to hold it", he embraced the young boy and proceeded to rub himself up against him, his genital area pressed into the nape of his back. Simon froze on the spot his arms held out reaching for the strings almost like an image in an old dilapidated photograph. Hugh momentarily released his grip as he leaned to switch off the light blowing and gasping as he did.

Still gripped with alarm Simon did not notice the darkness as he struggled to hold the banjo; he also did not notice that Hugh as well as removing his own trousers he

ideas and for the most part thoughts of this nature were largely ignored.

CHAPTER SEVEN

These images were planted firmly in his head as his mother called for him to remember to wash himself properly for church in the morning. He was also advised to pay particular attention to cleaning his ears when washing his hair, a rigorous challenge at the best of times and something he was loathe to do. He hesitated as he passed the brothers room were 'HS' was staying on his way to the bathroom, momentarily an apprehension filled him with dread similar to his fear of spiders.

The room appeared to be silent and he continued on his way. As he sat in the bath he remembered about his French homework and how his friend Stephen had promised to assist him with it; therefore on his to do list he resolved to call him on the telephone and remind him of his commitment. It was dark outside when he had finished bathing although it was still early enough to phone his friend. He went downstairs and entered the parlour where the telephone was situated and as he dialled his mother appeared from the living room.

"Are you ready for the morning?", she enquired in an unpleasant tone,

"looks like a nasty hangover" he uttered under his breath. -"Yes I'm just phoning Stephen about helping me with my homework tomorrow replied Simon",

"Okay straight to bed afterwards she said before retiring to the living room closing the door hard behind her.

Stephen answered the phone and they talked for ages about nothing; "listen Simon I shall not be able to come over tomorrow as my mum and dad are away for the weekend and I have to stay here. A bummer I know but what can you do, why don't you come here and we can help

each other, anyways my sister Lamia is here and she is excellent at French". "Okay fair enough that will do" he replied, "I need to get away from here for a while my mums in one of her long drawn out moods, I'll see you later."

Bridget as well as having binges of alcohol also had bouts of sobriety and while she was in this mode it was best to steer clear of her. She became very short tempered and would lift the nearest object to her and swing for you if you crossed her, Simon's present attitude was not in compliance with her restraint. He arose early the next morning got ready and went down to breakfast. His mother was at the table and he could tell by the look on her face she was not to be bothered with. Few words were spoken just enough to inform her that he was going to Stephen's after mass to revise his homework and he would not be home until later that night. Explanation complete he filled his school bag with the necessary books and disappeared out the door.

Simon sauntered along the road from his home that ambled through the flats complex, a road that resembled a hilled Valley leading onto a mountaintop. His first destination was to the church, then he was to continue on to the home of Stephen unlike just beyond. The roads around the complex, which sat in a basin, slithered, arched and twisted with the occasional hump rising and falling, much like the mountain streams etching their way downhill toward the sea.

As he walked in the early morning sunshine he listened to the chorus from the many birds that were seemingly perched on the rooftops of the pre-fabricated concrete dwellings. Most of the birds appeared to come from the sea, the main port situated a mere mile away. Their squawking and bickering going unnoticed by most of the land based variety, only noticeable whenever they tended to find the tiniest of scraps to eat. On such occasions they would battle like old fishwives at market for the shared crumbs.

Simon Sanders enjoyed taking this route not for the birds but for another attraction, situated in the sprawling balconies and pathways of the flats was a home bakery producing freshly made bread cut and uncut. Among many of its products there were rolls with a soft inner core with a crusty shell other wise known as the Belfast bap; numerous fresh cream, mouth-watering delicacies were also baked en masse. These produced aromas of yeast and barley that hung in the air for hours and always invoked a homely down to earth sensation, a smidgin of colour in a sea of grey.

He made it on time for the 11.am service and as he approached the chapel he saw the priest greeting those arriving. Father Mike Isfortune was an average size man of about 5"7 aged about 40 years and was blessed with an affable personality. However, once he got behind the pulpit the evangelical side emerged. His eulogies often concentrated on themes that were out there as far as Simon was concerned, quoting from the bible with regular sanctimonious fervour.

"Don't let anyone trick you with foolish talk, the lord God will punish those who disobey him so don't have anything to do with people who speak unwisely". As the father rambled on Simon listened intently, gripping every word, digesting it and trying to make sense of it. There was an obvious message, which carried ambiguous undertones, however, this was not clear to an impressionable young boy and for the time being he would remain bemused and unconcerned.

There appeared to be a certain pleasure also contained in the précis a detail he tended to relish. He condemned those who failed to turn up for Sunday mass as well as those who did. He cursed those who touched the demon alcohol rather than worship the lord. It was rumoured that parts of his sermons were based on confessions he had heard from the

confessional. Most Sundays a lot of people appeared to be red faced and embarrassed upon leaving after the service. This however did not deter a lot of people from attending.

Once the mass ended Simon made his way the short distance to his friends' home. Stephen Unlike lived with his parents and his two sisters in a detached house at the end of Coventree road. This house like the four, which were situated in their own cul de sac, were adorned with front and back gardens, a novelty as far as Simon was concerned.

Once inside the house Stephen suggested they have lunch before they started their revision. -

"not for me" replied Simon with a degree of modestly,

"why are you not hungry?" enquired his friend.

"Not really it is to early to eat",

As he spoke he noticed a football/soccer ball perched in the back garden invitingly waiting to be kicked.

"Lets have a kick around" Simon cried out as the two of them rushed out the back door and zoomed in on the sphere. All thoughts of revision disappeared as the boys frolicked around with the ball. The fun lasted for hours before their weary and tired bodies decided to have a break.

The two boys sat on a large tree stump located as it was on the perimeter of the large and spacious back garden. The remnant was huge similar to the top of a circular dinning table which fits snugly into the average kitchen eating area. The former tree that had maybe stood for decades had been unceremoniously chopped down, deemed unsightly by Stephen's parents. They sat in silence almost as if contemplating where to begin, their minds awash with happy pheromones often experienced after exertion and exercise before beginning to natter about all manner of topics.

Simon enquired about subjects in school, "which are your favourites?" he asked. Stephen pinpointed his hate for

French and science while Simon claimed to have a liking for all subjects, as he wanted to know all about everything.

"I have an interest in music and would like to be able to play an instrument of some kind," he informed his friend, "me to" replied Stephen.

"Really?", enquired Simon "what type of instrument interests you?"

"oh I don't know maybe the drums or the tin whistle, just something to blow in Sally Garden's face". One of the many girls at school who he disliked because of her ginger hair. Simon could sense a lack of seriousness in his friend's attitude and decided to hold back from his original assertion.

He began to explain how he would like to learn how to play the piano and of how he thought this instrument had mystical and magical qualities, as he described Stephen interrupted him in mid sentence.

"Lets go inside I'm hungry and dirty and I need to have a shower", and promptly made his way indoors. Simon followed making his way to the kitchen, which had an adjoining recreation area where the revision was to take place.

The extension had been created some years previous and added a certain quality to the property, as not only did it increase it's size adding value in the process it also provided easy access to the upstairs of the house.

"Go into the rec area and wait until I'm done then you can have a shower after," gestured Stephen. -

"What about your sister?" stuttered Simon in an uncomfortable tone.

"Who Lamia?, don't worry about her she is in her room mourning the loss of another boyfriend who has dumped her, in all probability crying her eyes out" indicated Stephen in a callous manner. He then proceeded into the bathroom slamming the door behind him.

Lamia at twenty-two was ten years older than Stephen and was educated to A level in French though that was as far as she took it claiming lack of interest. She stood about 5'7 had a fair complexion with piercing blue eyes. Her hair was black and she had a full and voluptuous figure. She also asserted she was to young to marry, although she was not wanton when suitor's came calling. According to Stephen who often complained about her and her crappy boyfriends she was always depressed and grumpy, "a typical girl" he called her. Simon had met her once fleetingly, just enough to realise her existence.

Simon retrieved his books and sat down for a spot of DIY French. The rec area was generous and roomy with a coffee table in the centre of the room and two large frumpy fluffy sofas facing one another running parallel with two bay size windows. Each was adorned with lace curtains that dropped the length of the window onto the floor giving the allusion of a bigger space. The effect of the curtains was such that anyone looking out through them was able to see a panoramic view, while those looking toward could only see white lace, a very apt device giving a modicum of privacy. The stairs led from the rec in an L-shape upwards with two levels onto the landing of the second story. The second story consisted of three bedrooms, a bathroom with adjoining toilet and an airing cupboard, a large house indeed for such a small family.

Simon busily studied his homework burying his head between the sheets of blotting paper. He was distracted by a commotion from the upstairs. Slowly he raised his head shifting his gaze accordingly, out of the darkness seemingly gliding on thin air walked the sister of his friend. Gracefully and with a certain finesse she elegantly stepped down the stairs stopping at the first landing where she perched herself onto the first rung.

He could see she was wearing a dressing gown with a pink negligee underneath and was barefoot. The gown was gently tied as she sat almost facing him, although she was about twenty feet away.

"Hello I'm Lamia," she whispered introducing herself in an imitation of supposedly French and English. As she did her gown gently and without fuss fell open revealing her undergarment, which barely covered her femininity. Simon answered with a grunt and a stammer as the beads of sweat began to dribble down his face and confusion swirled rampant in his mind.

Without uttering another word she raised her hips off the stair and eased the negligee up over her perfectly formed pelvis revealing a hirsute pantieless mid-drift. This appeared to stretch from her v to just below her nave as she tentatively and teasingly opened her legs a little bit further. With each movement she licked her lips in a seductive manner all the while eyeing him greedily.

Simon stared intently, intrigued by the vision before him. He had heard about the female form in biology class but this was a first and to add insult to injury he was totally unsure of his next move. He could hear clearly her faint groans as she purred catlike and beckoned him forth with her come to bed eyes - his natural instinct took over. Like the 'Satyrs' Pan, the ravenous demon of the forest he inched toward her, the stirrings in his underwear aching as he slithered his way forward.

He reached her position and he was overwhelmed with her scent, the aromatic fragrance of her perfume was all too powerful as she placed an arm around his neck caressing and stroking his hair between her nimble fingers. Simon was awestruck almost dumbstruck as he watched this picture of Venus in all her glory. He tried to speak but the words became entangled in the globules of saliva that his mouth now carried. She bade him to relax and gently

applied pressure to the back of his head directing him to her pulsating and somewhat drenched lips. He lent forward and she raised her hips slightly, as she did he took a full whiff and was almost overcome with excitement. He brushed past her inner thigh, his tongue ever so slightly touching her silky smooth by now moist skin. She gyrated and contorted onto his taste buds the vibration resonating and enveloping his entire mouth.

She squealed a little louder as she throbbed and gasped for air holding his head a little firmer. Moaning pleasurably her body tingling and trembling, yearning, in the throes of excitement. Tears of unspeakable joy welled in her eyes. She pressed his face against her area and with a certain amount of agility enclosed her ample inner thighs around his head. Simon gurgled and gagged with muffled groans almost suffocating with the mixture of saliva and essence.

The air was thick with the smell of sex as Lamia cloaked herself in mindless hedonism. She slowly and reassuringly gained her composure before realising she had a small problem lurking and it required attention. In the midst of her self-indulgence she had forgotten about Stephen who was preparing to leave the bathroom having finished taking a shower.

The sound of the door unlocking forced Lamia to release her young charge and like willow the wisp she was gone, disappearing back into her room as quickly as the west wind does blow and as quickly as she appeared. Simon Sanders meanwhile was left to comprehend the meaning of what just occurred, the momentum in his loins had not dissipated as he returned to his books. Subsequently after much reflecting and a cooling down period his attention was averted to French revision.

A short time later Stephen reappeared having dried himself and put on a change of clothing.

"What happened to you?" he asked, his friend noticing the agitated crumpled state he was in, his face beetroot red, his hair shagged and unkempt,

"nothing", replied Simon the agitation apparent in his voice and informed him it was very warm.

"Is it ok if I have a shower?", before going upstairs into the bathroom firmly locking the door behind him.

A plethora of confused thoughts whirled around in his underdeveloped brain as he stood under the showerhead. Without the consul and direction of a male figure in his life he was bereft of explanation.

"Is this how grown ups and children behave as they get older?" he pondered to himself; "same sex activity or male female relations?"

The scenario which now presented itself was perplexing, a conundrum he would have to resolve on his own, one thing seemed certain though his preference erred on the side of male, female relations.

CHAPTER EIGHT

Leaving the bathroom Simon's mood was sombre, his deliberations had left an imprint of morality on his psyche. His lack of understanding had forced him to question the rights and wrongs of decent behaviour. However, comprehension unnecessary he became aware of something not being right but was at a loss to pinpoint it. He informed his friend of his intention to give the revision a miss as he was worn out after the day's activities. He decided to walk home and hoped they would see each other at school the following day. He arrived home at dusk to an almost darkened house, a slight wind whispered through the large single tree positioned not far from his house and flickered over the small copse of bushes and hedges that marked the boundary of his home. As he strolled up the lane he could see two lights shining from two of the many windows. One was on in the kitchen were he knew his mother would be, preparing his favourite meal. It was Sunday and as far back as he can remember she always made homemade chicken and vegetable broth. as a starter to the main meal.

The soup consisted of barley and lentils that had been soaked overnight in a large pot, the carcass of a chicken was added along with a variety of other vegetables, carrots, peas and onions. This was seasoned with salt and freshly ground black pepper, all covered with water put on to boil, simmered, then allowed to infuse all the jewelled flavours producing a sublime soup. There was a distinct flavour attached to this which contained mothers secret ingredient but she refused to reveal it's content leaving everybody all guessing. A meal in itself his father used to say whenever he was there to taste it. While this was stewing she had already prepared the pot roast, which was slowly roasting in the

oven, the unmistakable aromas of Rosemary, and Thyme along with a hint of marjoram emanated from the kitchen. Roast and boiled potatoes, steamed carrots and freshly chopped Savoy cabbage sauté in garlic and butter accompanied the meal.

The other shining light came from the brothers old room where HS was staying the twang of his banjo echoed throughout the house as he played it profusely. Simon entered the hallway and the flavoursome aromas enveloped his senses, the allure guided his nose toward the kitchen.

He was welcomed by his mother who appeared to be in better form.

"Hello Simon how was your day studying with your friend?", she enquired pulling a chair away from the table enabling him to sit down.

"It was fine ma, we didn't get much done though, Stephen is not very academically minded all he prefers is to mess around he replied". "Well it is Sunday a day of rest and relaxation but it will do you good to get out of here for a while, your sister is resting in her room and might join us later if she is up to it". For a moment alarms bells began to ring in his head as he thought about Roberta alone in her room with 'him' in the house.

"Have you seen her today, has she had anything to eat?", his mother could see he was agitated about something.

"Calm down Simon, yes she has been down but you know her condition does not allow her to over exert herself. She watched some television had some lunch before retiring to her room". Bridget acknowledged his concern, however she also concluded that as a young boy soon to be a man he needed to have a life of his own, to grow up in his own world, to experience and enjoy childhood for as long as possible. He had had enough exposure to mature themes in his short tenure with the burden of his father's absence his

sister's illness and her on-off binges of alcoholic stupors. The challenge of adulthood was not far off.

Simon and his mother talked about a lot of subjects as they sat down to enjoy their meal, an experience he had missed for some time. They laughed and joked and he could see the smile on her face was making her feel alive again, their happiness ceased however as the appearance of HS changed the mood. "Something smells" tasty he declared as he made his way into the room. Bridget got up and invited him to supper and motioned Simon to set a place at the table,

"I'm not finished yet ma" he said and continued to eat not even bothering to raise his head to acknowledge his presence.

-"Simon Sanders don't be so rude that is no way to treat a guest".

His resentment was further heightened as HS nonchalantly pulled a chair and sat at the dinning table engaging his mum in non-sensical waffle.

"Any word from Robert?" he enquired,

"not so far" she enthused

"but I am expecting correspondence soon", adding that "she would be happy to have him home to relieve the burden on her hapless heart", poetically musing, the iambic pentameter skipping a beat. Simon arose from the table and placed his plate in the sink there was no need to scrape into the bin as he finished all that was put before him. There was a suggestion that he would have eaten the pattern as well had it been consumable. "Alright ma I'm off to my room eight o' clock comes early in the morning" he quipped referring to time he gets up for school; she bid him goodnight and off he went not bothering to give HS a second glance.

He climbed the stairs and suddenly felt the lethargy envelop his person the days events coupled with the large

meal just consumed began to have a sluggish effect on him, passing the room where 'he' had took up residence entering his own room closing the door firmly behind him. Standing there in what was for a fleeting moment his comfort zone thoughts of Lamia now raged. Untying and kicking off his shoes he fell onto the bed and not bothering to undress climbed under the sheets and succumbed to a restful sleep.

Sometime later he was awakened abruptly by someone manhandling him, "what time is it?" he said not knowing who he was addressing the sleep still firmly entrenched in his eyes. In the dark he could hear a voice hushing him the unmistaken waft of alcohol lingering in the air. Hugh had deftly and swiftly removed his trousers and underwear and was now toying with him. Simon's attempts at rejection were simply hushed away with "don't be shy it will be over soon". He got into bed beside him rubbing himself against the boy as he took his penis in his mouth. The shame and disgust of Simon was palpable with having excrement smeared on his face as he cringed at the touch of this vile man.

Closing his eyes and turning his head toward the wall the rape of his person continued. Suddenly HS was on his knees astride his chest attempting to insert his penis into the boys mouth, Simon's resistance was more determined however as he refused to submit to the will of this deviant monster. His reluctance an obvious sign of unwanted attention, yet and with swift aplomb he urged him to masturbate him force majeure. The absolute refusal forged an indefensible outcome as he groaned and yelped himself to conclusion.

His deed completed he crept out of his bed and stood in the dark regaining his composure. Simon meanwhile slipped under the covers as he did he caught a glance of this fiends silhouette outlined in the bleakness of night; the boy was undoubtedly frightened and alarmed by the vision before him. He observed and imagined this was a disciple of the

devil, Satan incarnate. He whispered to Simon "that this was their secret" and that he would be better off not saying a word to anyone placing a silver coin on his bedside table. Just like a slippery dog he skulked away into the darkness gently closing the door behind him so as not to alert anyone.

Simon lay in the darkness a flickering of moonlight struggled to penetrate through the flimsy curtains onto the dishevelled ambience of the room and it's contents. Feelings of isolation mingled with the cold and stillness, a miasma of confusion infiltrated his innermost thoughts. He had an inkling of something not being right, an uncertainly to explain the inexplicable where feelings of disillusionment and terror descended upon him.

He wished Billy or David were there, maybe even his father to explain his uncertainly and to enlighten him to the ways of man. His reasoning was edging toward telling his mother of the behaviour occurring in the room down the hallway from her and the monster in their midst, but what was he to say?. How could he illustrate the sordid conduct of a so-called Uncle, someone who had been invited into the family home. The guilt began to enwrap him, as he perceived the blame would fall on him for not doing more to stop the illicitly from happening. Either way he was uncomfortable in revealing this mans disgusting secret and vowed to stay silent. There was now a battle for his sanity-taking place, the tortuousness overwhelmingly intense as he tossed and turned on his emotional roller coaster. Suddenly he sat up and screamed out loud from the top of his lungs, the sound echoing throughout the house, the pent up emotion to great a burden for such small shoulders.

However as much as the sound resonated no one could hear his call, certainly not his mother who was intoxicated and asleep unable to decipher the actuality. Nor Roberta who could sleep undisturbed even as a philharmonic orchestra played outside her room. There was also a

question of how had he been heard what interpretation could be surmised. Would it have been recognised as a cry for help or just Simon having a bad dream, it seems in this current reality the latter was more creditable. The release of such a weight had the effect of allowing him to fall into a slumbering repose, the dark and blackness replacing the usual rapid eye movement. The next morning he was up at dawn and was first into the bathroom and as he stood under the slow dripping water from the large showerhead his contemplation reflected onto the previous nights events.

The water fell softly onto his head saturating his unkempt hair, seeping all the while down the back of his neck caressing gently his aching shoulders and back. It was then he came to a conclusion to confront his tormenter he was not going to be stifled any longer, his resolve firm and resolute. However well intentioned his defiance and bravado was his reluctance to speak back to his elders was absolute, a trait imbued in him by his father. Robert was of the opinion that children should be seen and not heard, ostensibly they should not question the authority and wisdom of their contemporaries. "Do unto those as you would have done to yourself, respect your mother and father and don't question their logic was the message he always professed".

Simon's adherence to this statement was profound, his behaviour and mannerisms often commended by those in authority, however there was a certain ambivalence attached as he began to question this same authority. He readied himself in front of the mirror vowing to face up to his intimidator and promptly left the bathroom to tell his charge where to get off. Approaching the room where the fiend was holed up he stopped at the door his stomach fluttering with butterflies as a shaking sensation enveloped his limbs. His nerves had turned to jelly and he imagined himself levitating, hovering looking down on himself.

"No going back now," he uttered and without knocking rushed through the door. He began to speak the words he had rehearsed earlier,

"right you listen to me you had better cut the crap and leave me alone", he said in one long monochrome sentence not stopping for breath. To his surprise the room was empty, no sign of the dreaded uncle or his belongings. The small bed with it's sheets and blankets neatly pulled back into a neat pile appeared as if no one had occupied it since the days of Billy and David.

Puzzlement now filled his thoughts along with a sense of shear relief. Could it be true did this unsavoury man pack his bags and just go? he could not tell. He turned on his heels to leave the room his intention to investigate further opening the airing cubicle door where extra bedding was kept and wet clothes were left to dry, to check in case he was in a state of somnambular.

Simon entered the kitchen and discovered his mother making him breakfast, "good morning son" she quipped her mood seemingly refreshed and at ease. "Back at you came" the reply as Simon pulled a chair at the table. She placed a plate of boiled egg and burnt toast in front of him apologising for the charred remains.

"So are we all set for a new week," she enquired,

-"yes ma I'm looking forward to getting back to school that was one long weekend",

"that's good I'm glad to hear," said Bridget.

"Incidentally, where is the lodger?" asked Simon in a blasé manner not wanting to appear to concerned.

"In his room I expect getting ready for the days toil", while she was speaking he interrupted telling her he was not in his room adding there was no sign of him and all of his belongings were gone.

"How do you know?", she asked.

"As I was passing the door was open I looked in and he was gone" Intrigued and surprised Bridget went to check herself. "Funny" she said on her return "no goodbye note or explanation". Mystified she assumed he had gone at dawn, as there must be problems with the construction of his house. "Glad to see the back of him" said Simon under his breath. "Well good riddance to him", he cried and lifted his bag over his shoulder and walked off to school.

CHAPTER NINE

Johnny, Stephen and Simon were seated in their English class chatting about the weekends events. As they waited on the 'masters' arrival Johnny enquired of them about the difficulties of the homework Mr Dory had given them the previous Friday; "homework", cried Simon, what homework?".

"Fishy Doc told us to write a 1000 word essay interpreting the book 'The old man and the sea", explained Johnny, "I can hear by your tone that homework was furthest from your mind Simon," he added with a wry grin.

"Well no, Stephen and I had every intention of completing our French together, however, we were distracted and played soccer all day Sunday and ended up so tired I just went home, English was not even on the list".

"That's a good way to start the week", said Johnny, "two pupils from the same class with non completed assignments, Fishy is going to love you".

"That is not a problem," explained Stephen "I have finished both homework's and still had time for breakfast";

"how did you manage that stammered Simon the words quivering and stuttering in his throat, you were as tired as much as I was?".

"Lamia assisted me, did I not tell you my sister was a French A level student when she was at school; I say she helped me when I should really give her all the credit as she done most of it which in turn give the time to finish English".

"That was awful decent of her," said Simon a hint of sarcasm hidden in his almost snivelling voice.

"Yes I know whispered Stephen", so as not to alert any of the class, "she claimed she could not sleep and insisted

on completing it for me". "Yes I wonder why", thought Simon his minds eye turning to Lamia, a picture of her hairy nakedness ingrained on his psyche, her smell still lingering in his nostrils.

"What about me?", moaned Simon;

-"I thought she did help you", supposed Stephen.

"No, no, no what do I tell fishy?"

"tell him the truth," said Johnny. -

"Yes that's right just tell him I was too busy playing soccer to even attempt his homework", cried Simon in a derisory fashion, "he'll hit me even harder". A look of bewilderment descended on all three as they tried to figure a way out.

"I know," said Simon drawing them both closer and softly speaking continued, "I'll explain that my sister took a turn for the worst at the weekend and my mind wasn't on the job",

"good one" uttered his friends.

The classroom door swung open it's handle striking the wall as fishy Doc swept strikingly and purposefully inside, his swaggering gate similar to that of someone of importance; his slender shoulders which appeared imposing under the oversize raincoat swayed gently to and fro, the coat tails dragged the surface of the floor tiles.

"Good morning Class, did we have a wonderful weekend completing our assignments", he said with an air of expectancy,

"yes" orchestrated his charges,

"good, come forth one by one in alphabetical order and place them in the in tray"; the pupils lined up single file forward as instructed and soon it was Simon's turn.

He approached and began to explain his predicament and his reasons for not completing his work. Fishy Doc's eyes narrowed his glared gaze focused on this unfortunate soul; he took him by the arm and told him to stand aside while

the remainder of the class handed in their work. The pupils returned to their respective desks in silence; Simon stood to the right of the master's desk just in front of his old rickety chair smiling in the direction of his friends. Mr Dory clearly exasperated paced back and forth just in front of the blackboard and slightly behind his desk rubbing his hands profusely, his mouth opening and closing as if he was gasping for air, similar to that of a drowning salmon.

"So master Sanders your sisters illness is the reason for not doing your homework", he said in more of a statement rather than a question the mockery apparent to all but Simon. The slowly shrinking boy shrugged his shoulders in acknowledgement as if to say yes but what can you do; fishy was having none of it however as he withdrew his strap from inside his coat and slammed it on the desk. The smile fell like tears from Simon's face as he was told to hold out his hands one on top of the other and be prepared for a shock; his protestations were ignored as he was told he knew the rules.

Flatly refusing to comply with Mr Dory's instructions he claimed he had a valid excuse,

"but sir, honest to God, there was to much commotion at home for an attempt at homework", the boys refusal incensed Mr Dory as he bellowed,

"how dare you use an illness in your family to explain away your

recklessness, I wont have it in my classroom, now hold out your hands". Again he refused staring ominously at his master, as beads of sweat formed on his forehead his nerves all-aflutter. Fishy was aghast at this pertinacious conduct and raised the strap in the air threateningly, almost as if he was going to strike the boy down before regaining his composure and returned to his pacing.

Simon who had been facing his teacher throughout the debacle turned his back to face the class looking at no-one

his gaze firmly fixed on the back wall. The only sound available was the creaking and moaning of the chair as fishy sat down, the silence comparable to that of an empty classroom as one and all looked on in silence at this ridiculous situation.

The frustration now turned to anger as Mr Dory seethed and writhed with furious anger, fumes of steam arose from his person. Without warning and reminiscent of Mount Vesuvius he leaped from his chair to an upright position, towering over the boy he lashed out striking him with the palm of his hand, the blow centring on the back of his neck just below his head. As he did he screamed

"blasphemous little imp!, you child of Satan, such impudence will not be tolerated in this class".

Simon was stunned and staggered unsurely on his feet almost collapsing to the floor. As the tears welled in his eyes a red mist descended in his mind, a hitherto unknown rage began to emerge; expletives of every nature spouted from his mouth, he swore and cursed this old curmudgeon.

"What the fuck, in the name of Jesus who to hell do you think you are, my father never hit me like that and you are certainly not going to, I'm getting out of this fucking class" and he rushed toward the door.

Fishy Doc seemed taken aback by the young Simon's retort and speedily reached the door before him. Blocking his exit, he urged him to calm down; Simon Sanders was having none of it though as he implored fishy Doc to allow him out of the room, his pleas turned to screams mixed with sobbing hysterics. When again his request was refused he began to lift the nearest thing to him, and throw at his master. Books, pencils, chairs even the old wobbly waste paper basket was tossed in his direction. Calm was only restored when a teacher from an adjacent classroom intervened claiming the whole school could hear the disturbance.

As the two teachers conversed Simon made his dash for freedom, out the door down the corridor and out of the school grounds. The seriousness of the situation was not lost on him as he settled in a nearby park to assess his options. What was he going to do now, how could he tell his mother of events. Although he was partly to blame there was no way in his mind he was going to be punished for something so trivial as not doing homework. Rules are there to be obeyed he understood but grievous bodily harm, he didn't think so.

He stayed in the park until dusk before making his way home, apprehensively creeping up the driveway with a sense of dread permeating his young bones. He assumed the school would have telephoned his mum to inform her of the situation and to evaluate and ascertain what measures to take in dealing with her unruly son.

However on entering the home he was greeted by the sound of his mother's music, which was being played softly and gently in the front room. He hung his coat on a rail behind the door and dumped his schoolbag in the corner before entering the room where the music was emanating. It was a familiar sight his mother 'drunk' sitting on the sofa sobbing quietly while listening to her mournful dreary music. "That's good" he thought, "they either have not contacted her or they have and she had been oblivious to the call", regardless this would give him some breathing space to decide on a creditable excuse. He left the room bypassing the kitchen where he could hear the small portable television on indicating Roberta was there and without supper went upstairs into his own room gently closing the door to advert attention to himself.

Sitting in the darkness his thoughts were drawn to the day's events and how totally out of character his actions were. Even with all the turmoil with mother he had never before raised an eyebrow or had a malicious thought. He lay

down on the bed, his young mind full of torment, questions of why had he become so aggressive infiltrated his head and toyed with him. "This cannot be a normal situation, adults do not interact with children to such a degree" he mused referring to the actions of 'Hugh and Lamia'. His astuteness now more apparent he became aware of the evil, which happened against him and determined to stop it ever occurring again as slowly he drifted off to sleep.

While he was in REM land his dreams became more disturbing and lifelike almost as if they actually happened. In one of them he was being chased by a pack of vicious wild Rottweiler dogs along a high plateau that reaches just below the clouds in the sky. As they neared him he came across a sheer cliff that dropped into a bottomless crevice, with nowhere to go he leaped into the clouds flapping his arms as if he were a bird. As he drifted downward at a terrific speed he thought he should be wearing a parachute and when one appears on his back his relieve is long winded. This fails to open when he pulls on the rip cord and he disappears into the blackness with the dogs gnashing at his heels.

Struggling in the darkness he emerges into a wooded bog where he comes face to face with little troglodytes who appear in male and female forms, a chase ensues. Galloping in the opposite direction he is running but not moving, his arms and legs flailing in the wind. Suddenly he lands in a pit of quicksand and begins to sink, screaming in terror as he slowly goes under. To add to the horror he is joined by the demons as they pull and tear lumps of flesh from his body. His horror completed when the Rottweilers drag him by the heels into oblivion. After each unsettling dream he awakes with a sudden jolt a cold sweat enveloping his body. "Freaky and eerie", he thought to himself but quickly forgotten as he arose to face another day.

CHAPTER TEN

The kitchen was empty and he proceeded to make himself some breakfast. Once he was finished he grabbed his bag and went off to school along the way he pondered how he was going to rectify things or even if it was at all possible to put things right, he wouldn't know until he faced the music. Walking on the edge of town towards his school he saw a boy the same age as himself who he recognised from primary school.

Samuel Sercal (he preferred to be called Sammy) had been a peripheral figure at school and had rebelled at an earlier stage in his development. At 5`7 he was tall for his age towering over all other children. Although slim he was blessed with a full head of blond hair with a peculiar shape to his eyes in that their appearance suggested he gazed through slit like openings with pronounced eyebrows that ran in a straight line across his forehead. He was afflicted with a squelched lisp and was often the butt of other pupil's amusement, "alwaycs aslking did he scpeak sctrange".

His father was unknown and he lived alone with his mother who for one reason or another could not control him. Sammy was a below average student who showed little interest in education, his mother concurred and never bothered sending him there. This in effect was leading him astray possibly into a life of crime and wantonness, not the kind of person Simon cared to bother with. However his free and liberal nature now took on a new resonance and an intrigued Simon Sanders choose to get to know him better.

Throwing caution to the wind he approached Sammy who was idling, loitering about doing nothing in particular.

"Alright, what's the crack?" he enquired coyly,

"oh nothing mucsh" came the reply, "just waiting for old man Bumpkin to turn his back so I can grab one or two of those apple's".

He was referring to Bumpkins fruit and vegetables, a grocery store at the bottom of Ladymar road. It was a firm favourite of a lot of students and teachers and was often very busy at lunchtime. A large trestle table adorned the shop front and was covered with a mat of fake grass consisting of faded colours of green and light brown. On top were cardboard boxes filled with apples, oranges peachces and pear'cs. Small barrel shaped containers cut in half were filled with potatoes, turnips, parsnips, Savoy and white cabbage all lumped together for maximum display. On entering the shop the smell of sea salt and freshly caught fish of the trout and salmon variety circulated and enveloped the senses, overlapping was the sweet aroma of garlic and smoked Italian sausage. A fine little delicatessen filled with deliciousness for the discerning palate, as well as catering for the sometimes ruff and gruff of the uncaring uncivilised taste of the pubescent type.

Sammy was waiting for the chance to steal some apples for his breakfast once old man Bumpkin became pre-occupied. The arrival of Simon increased his prospects, as old Bumpkin was unfamiliar with him, unlike Sammy.

"He knows me", whispered Sammy and urged Simon to swipe the biggest and most juiciest looking apples,

"grab those big ones they will last longer and are more filling," he said in an experienced tone, urging him on, willing him to steal.

The trepidation was palpable as he inched forward toward the display his fear soon replaced with excitement as a million butterflies tumbled around his belly, he lifted two big round firm green apples and quickly walked away. He heard a yelp of euphoric glee as he made his way down a

side ally leading behind the shop. Sammy joined him and the two greedily ate their spoil.

"Well done" gasped Sammy "I didn't think you had it in you".

"Ach' it was wee buns" replied Simon his face red with excitement; "I could feel a shutter run down my spine, I thought my heart was going to burst it was beating so fast". He had experienced his first thrill of the chase, an adrenaline pumping sensation flooded his veins and he felt good about it, all of his worries disappeared and he wanted more.

"So Simon what is your crack, are you not the teachers pet in school?" enquired his new found friend.

"Hardly, I have an interest in gaining knowledge and a thirst for understanding, I enjoy school it beats hanging around this crappy place; and don't you know knowledge is power" retorted Simon, the effrontery clearly obvious in his tone.

"Well I don't know much about those big words but I am going into town to see what else I can lay my hands on, what about it?", said Sammy, his words implicit in their candour. Simon stood in silence as he pondered the situation, part of him was edging toward school, part of him seduced by the illegality of following his deviant friend even though now he too could now be classed as a thief having participated in a misdemeanour. In the end the thrill seeking was too strong to resist and he followed his teacher, the leash tied loosely around his neck.

Over the coming months and years the two became close partners in crime, albeit crimes of a trivial nature, stealing mainly food, fruit and Vegetables. However the vegetables were often discarded as there was nothing less appealing than raw carrots and celery sticks.

One of their favourite activities was hopping; this entailed chasing after large lorries, vans and buses, waiting

until they stopped at traffic lights or simply slowed down and hitching a ride; a sort of quest for excitement on the long days playing truant, on the beak or simply skipping school. While extremely dangerous it was an essential ritual for unruly adolescents who would stand on the corners watching the traffic as the challenges were made.

"Right Simon there is one there try and get on the left hand side of that big dumper truck," said Sammy Sercal.

If anyone knows what these trucks looked like they would have understood the anxiety building in the central nervous system of Simon Sanders.

"Jesus", murmured the challenged, "that thing is enormous, I don't know if I'll be able to reach the bottom lip of the trailer never mind the left hand side of it". Simon finally sensed the fear gene, became reluctant and suggested waiting for a better opportunity.

"Ah cut the crap," hollered Sammy Sercal, "if you can't do this one then you are a yellow belly and I will have to think again about our friendship. Don't be thinking for one moment that I won't be telling the rest of the boys about your cowardice, you may get your boots on and get after that lorry if you want to be in my gang".

Simon could feel and taste his sweaty palms as a warm uncomfortable heat enveloped him, his anxiety levels went into overdrive as he prepared to face this leviathan of the construction industry. He watched as the big twelve wheeled lorry pulled up slowly to the red traffic light, and as rain falls on a window pane the sweat built on his forehead before slowly trickling vertically along his brow.

"Go, go, go now", cried Sammy "the light is about to change if you don't go now you are going to miss it". Simon darted out onto the road, zig zagged through the traffic and leap onto the right hand side of the monster truck. He managed to grab hold of a handle protruding from it's side and secured his stand. The driver, as was so often

the case caught a glimpse of his unwanted passenger and place his foot on the accelerator, as the lorry gained momentum Simon started to feel his grip release due to the water now pooled in his palms. His ordeal was just beginning and he felt the fear well in his eyes and heart, the blood in his body rushed through his veins and he could feel and hear it as it pulsated and throbbed over his brain.

"Jesus Christ" screamed within, "I'm going to die, fuck Sammy Sercle and his code of conduct. If this is what it takes to get accepted then I'd rather be alone".

Then just as he dammed all to hell he felt the motion of the lorry ease as it came to another set of lights, fortunately the red was blazing and the demon truck pulled up and stopped. Jumping down from his perch he caught sight of the driver's face in the mirror, he appeared to be smiling and rubbing his hands, reminiscently.

Walking back to where his so called buddy was waiting for him he tried to regain some sort of composure his inner voice raged, "well that's it, no more of that shite, Sammy Sercle can run on if he thinks I'm doing that again".

Approaching his original spot he could hear the yelps of Sammy as he wailed, "well done our kid you passed the test".

Simon Sanders tried to hide his annoyance in a smile all the while thinking "fuck you".

Soon Simon was introduced to a few of Sammy's other miscreant friends. There was Malcolm the skunk so called for obvious reasons, his unwashed odour stained person leaving a lot to be desired. There was a suggestion going around the camp that something had crawled inside his body cavity where items are discarded and died, the festering decomposing stench emanating from every pore in his body. Tucker the fucker allegedly sold his young soul to the devil; would sink you as quick as he looked at you,

cared only about his own interests, often stealing to feed his own habits, though still hung around like a bad smell.

Jake the snake who slithered around enticing young women with pieces of gold and silver into showing him their underwear and was very successful in his endeavours. Ricky tricky dickey McNoon with his obese stature would often blunder into larger shops filling his pockets with anything that could fit. Always managing to allude the law putting the finger on some other unfortunate; a most distasteful and dodgy bunch of characters who would stop at nothing for cheap thrills. The ultimate school of scoundrels, for his part Simon was nicknamed brains probably because he was the only one with a semblance of education, the voicse of reascon Sammy called him.

Meanwhile back at home Simon's corrupt activities reached a crescendo as he carried on his downward spiral into unlawfulness. He completely disregarded anything his mother demanded, ignoring his duties and his responsibilities especially toward his sister. His appearance had become unkempt and his attitude uncouth, his personal hygiene neglected. He started to experiment with smoking cigarettes thinking it was cool and sophisticated to walk around with a stick of death hanging from his mouth.

All the while never realising the damage he was inflicting on himself, his health already showing signs, whizzing in his chest and a shortness of breath. Another drawback was the condition of his teeth that had become stained yellow, his breath already smelling like an ashtray as was the clothes he wore. His descent was almost complete, his schooling had become secondary and his adherence to the rules nonexistent, there was only one way to go from here and little did he know the consequences, nor did he care.

CHAPTER ELEVEN

Simon had just celebrated his fifteenth birthday when an event occurred that changed everything that went before. He and his so-called friends used to hang out at a small café when they weren't out stealing or causing mayhem; Pablo Uriah's famous for its fruity curry served hot and cold drinks, chips and the popular beef burgers and cheese burgers, often these were the only sustenance many of the youths ate. A major attraction of this small eatery was the pinball machine where everybody competed against each other to achieve the highest score. It became so in demand that the owner seeing a further money making opportunity offered prize money of a £1 if the highest score went unbeaten for week, Simon was good at this but there was always somebody better.

The shop was about 12ft square, room enough for two small tables and chairs and the pinball in the corner, a large front window with the owners surname emblazoned across it in flashing neon lights lighting the cold evening nights. It was also a place where most of the skulduggery was concocted, moves and robberies were discussed over strawberry and vanilla milkshakes. A favourite activity was stealing cars and when one evening their attention was drawn to noise outside Uriah's they all went to investigate. Sitting there in a large flashy white car was Tricky dickey McNoon in the drivers seat, Sammy along side him in the passengers seat. There was another figure in the back seat that, he could not get a clear look at. Sammy waved to him indicating he should come and join them, without hesitation off he went.

"what's happening, who owns this?" he said, the pangs of excitement rippling in his voice.

"Never mind," said Sammy "just get in we'll tell you later", and without a second thought he jumped into the back. Tricky dickey sped off up the Grosvenor road in the direction of the mountains and as he approached speeds of almost 100 kph along the small country roads clipping the branches of overhanging trees the hedge groves brushing the side of the car dangerously Simon was informed of the plan.

The car had been stolen from a car park in the town of Mastergeehy some ten miles away by 'Turkey neck Larry' a cousin of Tucker the fucker. Turkey neck was introduced to Simon who quickly informed him his name was Lawrence Dimonn but he preferred to be called Larry,

"why is he called turkey neck?" enquired Simon,

"you'll see" came the reply out of the darkness. Apparently Larry had broken into the car after had seen a package on the floor of the foot well of the passenger side. Once inside the car the ignition keys fell from behind the sun visor above the driver's side and he promptly sped off in it. "Cool or what" Larry blurted out and they all had a great laugh about it.

His investigation of the package revealed an unloaded handgun which Larry now held in his lap. As Simon looked at him he saw his eyes narrow and his lip curl as he uttered out of the side of his mouth his neck protruding from out of his shirt collar

"this is going to make us a fucking fortune", he said pointing to the gun, bemused Simon looked at Sammy and asked, "how?".

"Well our kid," replied Sammy "there is a little shop just up the road here and we are going to rob it",

"wi, wi, we?" stammered Simon "what do you mean we". "I don't mind stealing fruit and other Mickey mouse stuff but armed robbery you'll get fourteen years in prison for that".

"Don't worry about it," said Larry "we'll be in 'GIVE ME THE MONEY' and out in a flash".

"Yeah" chirped up tricky dickey "we'll be in and out before anyone knows we were there, this car is a flying machine". Unconvinced Simon sat in the back of the car weighing up his options the futility of it all played heavy on his mind.

"So when am I going to get to drive this monster"?, he enquired after a long pause.

"Anytime you want" Tricky Dickey said with a snigger, the evil intent evident in his manner.

"Hold on a minute" stuttered Sammy Sercal, "I never knew you could drive Simon, this is too powerful a car to fuck around in".

"What" cried Simon "if you think I'm getting involved in this hair brained scheme without a few thrills myself you can think again and anyway it will be a tester for the next job". "N-nexct job" uttered Sammy Sercal; "yes next job the one after this if it's successful, better to have two drivers just in case a problem crops up". "Point taken" came the reply from Tricky Dicky as he pulled the car over to the road side verge.

Sitting in the drivers seat placing his hands on the small sports steering wheel the excitement was obvious in Simon as unknown to him the natural endorphins produced in his brain flooded his body making him tremble.

"Right now take it easy," exclaimed Sammy Sercal "we don't want any foolish moves here just cruise on around the road there at a steady speed no need for heroics".

"Fuck that" retorted Turkey Neck Larry "by the time we get there the shop will be closed, let him take it round or somebody else take it".

"I like your style" laughed Simon and took off spinning the car's rear wheels burning rubber as he did. - "Whoa! slow down" raged Sammy Sercal who by this time had been

banished to the back seat as Tricky dickey now occupied the front.

"Go on ye lad ye" quipped Turkey neck "that's how you do it we'll be there in no time", slipping a stick of gum into his mouth and chewing profusely as his excitement grew. Suddenly the sound of wailing sirens pierced the night and all four of them turned toward the back window to witness in the distance but gaining fast were the flashing blue lights of a police patrol car.

"What the fuck? cried Simon, the cars obviously been reported stolen, we're fucked". "Not to worry" said tricky dickey "they will never catch us in this, just relax keep your eyes on the road and whatever you do keep a constant speed".

The small roads were not intended for cars travelling at rally speeds as the stolen car moved along them increasing in speed and purpose. At intervals along the route there were natural humps where the road rose and fell like a giant sperm whale rising for air before slowly descending into the depths. These did not deter him though as he raced to them at speed the car rising and lifting on all four wheels as he attempted to negotiate their idiosyncrasies. As the driver yelped and yahooed with excitement the blood from the other occupants drained from their bodies and now pooled on the floor, their faces ashen with fear.

Then worryingly, from around a distant corner in front of them came the lights of another police car, it raced toward them headlights and blue lights flashing, Simon yelled, "ye ha lets play chicken". Sammy told him to slow the fucking car down as he was going to get them all killed but it was obvious this boy was on a suicide mission. Then out of nowhere on a slight bend stood in the middle of the road a figure all in black, no one knew why he was there nor seemingly did they care.

As the headlights caught him Simon could see it was an old man and he appeared to be waiting to be hit by the car.

"Watch that ould boy," cried the occupants as bedlam now ensued in the mire,

"fuck him", murmured Simon, as an apparent death wish took hold and he made no attempt to avoid him. The car intentionally smashed into the pedestrian and sent him flying at least fifty feet into the air landing in a slump in the road as the offending car speed off on it's journey. Pandemonium erupted as the three passengers pleaded with Simon to slow down and stop the car so they could flee across the fields making good their escape into the night.

"No way lads cant do that the police car is right up our arses we'll get caught if we stop now". Sure enough the police car was gaining fast as they watched it swerve to avoid the lump in the road. -"You had better stop this car you fucking manic," cried the three.

"Why did you do that"? asked Sammy Sercal "he was standing plain as the nose on your face I saw him and I'm in the back seat". Nonchalantly and without remorse Simon replied, "I didn't see the old fucker, he just appeared out of the blue", what would you have preferred me to do drive into the field and get stuck in the mud"?

As the next bend approached Simon pressed down on the accelerator as the car went into a tight curve and then as it came onto a straight another police vehicle heading toward them rammed into the front of the stolen car.

The impact was spectacular as steel upon steel collided with sparks and windscreens dispersing in all directions, the shattered glass mingling with broken bulbs and headlights. A resounding crunch infiltrated the coolness of the night the cries for help sent crashing to oblivion as falling leaves drift on the wind. Four officers were slightly injured and were treated at the scene for mild shock, the boys however

suffered more serious injuries and were transferred to hospital.

Sammy Sercal was flung out the back window and was killed instantly. Larry had to have three fingers on his left hand removed as they were damaged when his hand was mangled along with the car door. Tricky dickey McNoon in the force of the impact went straight through the front windscreen and was decapitated. Simon's condition was unknown however as he was knocked unconscious in the collision. And as he was not responding to any stimuli it was difficult to determine the extent of his injuries.

The police informed Bridget the next day about her son's situation and since his absence went unnoticed from the home she seemed somewhat unconcerned. It appeared that because of his uncontrollable behaviour she had given up on him and she could say hand on heart, none of her other brood ever brought the authorities to her door. All of these negative emotions vanished on witnessing her youngest son laying on a hospital bed with tubes inserted in his nostrils and a saline drip attached to his arm.

He looked so helpless and fragile in his state of suspended animation she thought his loneliness palpable with her own. The doctors informed her that he was in a forced coma having received a serious knock to his cranium on impact. They were unsure of how long this state would last explaining that any brain injury was extremely serious and all they could do was let nature take its course. "The complexities of modern medicine", she mused as she held his hand fixing the sheets to make him more comfortable.

At home she searched out her phone book containing contact numbers for her husband and her son, David's location was unknown, she had no way of letting him know of the situation. She didn't care to disturb Robert with trivial chit-chat so never bothered to ever contact him but this was different she thought he needed to know. Finding

her book she at first telephoned her husband who informed her he would be home as soon as circumstances would allow. William told her he would be on the next train. The next day at the hospital when she arrived to visit her son she observed a stranger sitting by Simon's bedside, he stood to greet her and she vaguely recognised his face. He informed her he had heard about the accident on the radio and thought the name of the injured party familiar.

"Thanks for the concern but who are you?" replied Bridget.

"Oh I'm so sorry my name is Gabriel O Deus I went to school with David", the rasping sound of his voice making her feel instantly at ease.

"I can't recall you", added Bridget "but you are more than welcome to stay"

At that Billy arrived and made his way to his younger brother's side. As they all stood around the bed the doctor updated them on his progress,

"his condition is stable but we can see a slight improvement", and as he was speaking Gabriel interrupted and said, "all we can do is pray".

Billy turned to his mother and asked, "who was this character preaching".

"Why this is David's friend surely you must remember him from school replied Bridget".

"Not really" said Billy "I can't recall it was so long ago".

Apologising he offered his hand to Gabriel as a sign of friendship, as both men shook Gabriel whispered "don't worry I remember you".

'It is times of crisis that a re-emergence of faith develops, where people facing hardship and despair turn to their church for comfort and solicitude. They pray to some unknown entity in the hope their requests are answered; this

is particularity prevalent in the Roman Catholic faith where a trinity of rosary are often said beseeching their God for redemption and favour'.

CHAPTER TWELVE

The Sanders family were Catholics, however, they were not practising and had allowed their faith to lapse; and although Simon would attend mass on a Sunday it was through choice and not necessity. It was considered clichéd and people usually always had some excuse for not attending, either some had not or could not find the time or that their beliefs had changed or simply they could not be bothered. But like every trite conception the circle completes its revolution, similar to learning to drive a motor vehicle once you pass you never forget.

The family took the advice of Gabriel and retreated to the small room converted into a church by the hospital not as one might think for the benefit of the Sanders but for visitors, patients and anyone who wished to gather their thoughts.

As they prayed Bridget received a welcome surprise when Robert arrived at the door; he gesticulated for her to join him out in the corridor where he sought an update on his son's status. After a brief embrace and a simple kiss on the lips he was informed of the situation, with a shrug of the shoulders and a sigh of relief he uttered that he wouldn't wish the emotions of a teenager on anyone. Somehow suggesting the angst of adolescents with their ever changing bodies filled with testosterone charged ions was the cause of his misery.

The situation at the hospital remained the same and Simon's condition continued on its slow but stable recovery. One calendar month had passed and although he was out of danger he had not regained consciousness there still was the steady stream of well wishers and concerned others visiting him on a nightly basis as well as the ever

smiling presence of Gabriel O Deus. Although always remaining in the background he was always quick to offer words of comfort making everyone feel at ease with his radiance.

Billy conversed with his father and mother on a number of issues searching for a connection to Simon's reckless behaviour. Father and son were of the opinion that Bridget's hard drinking was a major influence, it was the main reason why Billy moved out of the family home at the earliest opportunity and why Robert felt the need to be away working all the time. However because it was such a contentious and emotive issue they never conveyed their feelings to the wife and mother, skirting the topic deeming it to touchy a subject.

Bridget unaware of the ill-feelings directed toward her considered the absence of a father figure at home a factor in her sons behaviour the drinking a response to her loneliness and despair. The debate raged on almost secretively in whispered tones of a hush when suddenly Simon's eyes flickered open. As he scanned the room his opaque vision slowly became clear as all in the room gasped with sighs of relief hugging each other and quietly thanking God for answering their prayers. There was however a sinister development occurring that would have family and doctors in a dilemma.

As Simon sat up all he could see were strangers and figures of unknown origin. As he looked at the faces staring back at him he was unable to discern any notable persons, his mother, his father even his brother appeared alien to him, the portion of his brain responsible for memory failing to make a connection. He began to get agitated and frightened his confusion raised to the highest levels and when he attempted to speak all he could muster was a whimper. And while unable to speak he did indicate by scribbling on a piece of paper that he required a Turkish

Delight, a small confectionary bar of jelly and chocolate coating, which to Simon's confused palate tasted cool and refreshing. Although the process of speech and vocalization was unable to materialize, to the doctors theory this was progress.

Bemused the anxious mother and father sought answers from the doctors, who, equally baffled could only offer the probable prognosis of a temporary brain malfunction brought on by blunt force trauma not uncommon with such perceived head injuries. Robert considered this explanation insufficient and probed the doctors for a more compelling answer. After much deliberation when he was filled with half truths and speculation he came away non the wiser. The best they could offer was that time will run its course, it could take weeks, months or years they just did not know, the complexities of the human mind were infinite one doctor concluded.

Simon's rehabilitation had commenced, his journey would be long and arduous, a venture into the unknown the destination uncertain. Physically all his parts functioned properly, his arms, hands, fingers and thumbs perfect, his legs, knees and ankles all worked normally. The problem lay in his perception of reality as his mental abilities were flayed and shattered. His brain was mush, although still a sponge he was incapable of gathering and processing information even in its simplest form.

Temporary amnesia and vocal misalignment were to be treated by the hospital psychiatrist and a speech therapist respectively, however after weeks of little change he was sent home to recuperate. While in familiar surroundings he did regain a knowledge of who he was and a recollection of those close to him, his progress was similar to that of an infant taking their first steps and uttering their first 'mama' or 'dada'. A truly frustrating experience not only for Simon but for the family as a whole.

The situation remained constant for approximately two years and in that time Simon made a slow and steady recovery, his speech returned albeit with a slur its tempo similar to that of a record playing at 33 revolutions per minute. And while his short term memory, a part of the brain where recent events are stored for easy recollection, was repressed he still possessed access to his long term memory. A process where events from earliest childhood to occurrences from as far back as yesterday, are stored deep in the brain in a region called the hypothalamus and are usually recalled subconsciously. Simon had trouble correlating events long term although they were still swirling recklessly in his mind, his short term memory was blank.

A cavernous darkness now existed where once there was light, almost as if part of his life had been wiped clean, like a disk clean up command on a computer once activated it is hard to replace data. He did however have portions of memory return to him in flashback, some were pleasant like eating his mothers favourite dinner when he imagined the aroma of the roast chicken hovering and the intermingling of the herbs rosemary and thyme smothered in sumptuous gravy, the salivating juices dribbling as he thought. But for the most part the flashbacks contained images of a disturbing nature. Most of his time was occupied in trying to establish some sort of identity, of discovering his raison d'être in the grand scheme of things.

Sitting in his room he looked out the window at the naturalness of the sky and it's constant moving and changing; dark coloured clouds yielding to grey coloured clouds. He could see entities, forms and shapes appearing and disappearing, his allusions allowing him to imagine winged Angels hovering, shining a light on his tortured mind. Slowly they would descend through the ether joining him at his side, massaging his neck, gently stroking his

temple with nimble fingers, comforting, a blanket of cloud with sporadic gaps of openness peering into the blue beyond, mesmerizing his wounded brain.

The occasional flashback appeared and disappeared, shooting across his forehead like a meteor, it's luminous spark igniting realisations; managing to grasp one of these stars the memory started to flood. It centred on a period when his rebellious phase was in full swing, when he and others used to go hopping traffic.

He remembered being alone walking, searching for his companions and there appeared a big red double Decker bus, the old London style type. Anyone with a bit of nerve could race along behind it jump on the small platform at the rear and swing on the chrome support bar, the shininess and sparkle of the bright steel was very attractive. Simon Sanders clambered aboard this mode of transport and smiled at his success; he swung round the bar, as a child swings around on a rope tied to a tree, at that moment the bus passed a stop sign and unable to avoid or unaware of the sign he smashes face first into it. The momentum of the bus carried on and he was flung in a backward motion to the ground. Laying on his back with confused thoughts all around he struggled to understand what just happened, "Jesus Christ did I just hit that pole there?", swirled in his scrambled thoughts, precariously he struggled to his feet and made his way home.

In his reverie he was unsure of what was real or fantasy, were the visions he was experiencing based on actual footage?, or just the ruptured synaptic junctions repairing themselves; sending thoughts and probabilities along the connectors to add to the confusion. One thing was real for sure though, he had lost four teeth from his bottom jaw and a steel plate was inserted to hold the frame together, he had slight double vision in his left eye; this carried a troubling aspect, he just could not recall the origin of these injuries.

Unpleasant images of HS were never far from the surface and concentrated on a male performing disgusting act of a sexual nature on him but because he had no memory of these events occurring he put them down to nightmares. Memories of Lamia's behaviour was less distressing however as these tended to put him into a state of arousal "quite pleasing and refreshing" he thought, whenever he experienced them, but still he put these down to the dream process.

A lot of the imagery occurred during sleep and it was sometimes difficult for him to separate reality from fantasy. One such dreamlike situation had him walking through a field of flowers, daffodils and tulips the colours of yellow and purple enhanced.

He comes across a large bull and as he focuses on it the sky turns dark shading the flowers black. Its demoniacal crimson coloured eyes fix a gaze as it speaks out of the side of its mouth 'alright my son' and grins at him. Frightened he turns to run but before he does a large phallus covered in cobwebs drops from between its legs, dangling. On seeing this he sprints across the field through the trees where he then comes across three human like figures with hoods on their heads worshipping a large three dimensional cross. This in turn is flashing with colours of red, blue and green. The figures lift him on top of the cross and begin to shout obscenities at him, -"you fucking bastard, you cunt of a person, you waster of living flesh"; he then falls head first into a deep crevice before waking in a confused state.

This was his existence, constant dreams and nightmares and thoughts of total inadequacy, gone was his confidence, his gregariousness, his well being. Replaced with paranoia and feelings of not belonging of being under threat from everyone he came into contact with. There was no psychiatric help offered to guide him through this mire of uncertainly no-one to hold his hand to offer reassurance

His father had returned to work as did Billy surmising his recovery almost complete, although Robert did leave word that he was to be kept under constant supervision. Bridget had managed to curb her alcohol intake while her husband was around, however with his leaving it returned with gusto.

CHAPTER THIRTEEN

A semblance of normality descended on the Sanders household the tiny nuances of behaviour once so prevalent now replaced the lethargy, which had enveloped everyone since the accident. Roberta's condition was stable and she was able to carry on with life without much mishap. Simon had returned to school, however this seemed pointless as he had missed so much and there was only one term remaining. This was a further burden on him as he missed out on acquiring the basics needed for dealing with the prospect of adulthood. As he was later to discover education and learning were not the only products provided through schooling, essential life skills and societal bonding was also achieved - although for now he was just glad to be alive. The old Simon had returned albeit missing a few faculties and he was ready to enter into the fray of the real world, however if he thought this was going to be easy he could not have been more wrong.

He met his first true love when he fell for a pretty young woman who would spend the next five years with him. Lucy Ferrier at seventeen was one year younger than him and had all the qualities he admired, dark auburn hair, piercingly seductive blue coloured eyes with a body not quite fully developed but with ample proportions. Her personality was in complete contrast to his, shy and introvert with never much to say, what she did possess, however was the ability to curb Simon's moody and sometimes reckless behaviour.

It wasn't long into their relationship when she discovered his affliction. He was prone to uncontrollable mood swings and temper tantrums especially when they were alone together. He would snap at her disparagingly for

no particular reason accusing her of being unfaithful, conniving and whispering behind his back. She however was quickly on the defensive calming the situation and soothing his fears her voice of reason penetrating deep into his psyche. A modern day 'Titan Themis'; keeping order and control.

Simon was her suitor for three years before he thought of asking her to marry him and when he did she accepted without hesitation even though she was aware of his flawed moods, which continued sporadically. A long engagement ensued and after another long year there was still no sign of a wedding day. For her part Lucy was just happy she could tell her friends she was not quite hooked.

The situation was not really pressing on Simon he just did not see the urgency of settling down they were still quite young and had plenty of time; he loved her deeply but the time did not appear to be right. He had managed to find employment as a construction labourer excavating drainage pipes with a pick and a shovel and clearing away the muck from the sewage system, a poorly paid and backbreaking vocation; his mind was constantly bothered with 'what if?'....

He often thought when he was knee deep in excrement and urinal waste of how different life could have been had he not chosen the path he did. If he had taken the punishment of 'Fishy Doc' for not during his homework his life might well have turned out more prosperous. Or had he just continued on to school that day instead of hooking up with Sammy Sercle he was sure he would have a more meaningful job earning a decent living, driving a reliable car with a plush house in the suburbs.

"Hindsight" is hopeless he muttered to himself "it only brings on depression". This was another reason for not marrying Lucy his reluctance was spared on by his deficiency in standing, what sort of life could he give her

with such a menial job. How were they to settle down and raise a family. However despairing, Simon ever the eternal optimist always held out hope.

Simon arrived home from work on a bitterly cold October night in his usual state cold, angry and tired, and to add to his misery his mother called out reminding him not to enter the house in his present state. Begrudgingly and unapologetically he stomped around the back of the house to the tool shed where he was to decontaminate himself and discard his work clothes. In normal circumstances when the working man returns kicks off his boots, washes for supper and slumps in front of the television tired and frail did not apply. The stench emanating from Simon was similar to that of rotting food; it percolated his pores and carried on the wind, he had to be fumigated spending on average an hour in the bathroom washing himself down.

"I don't know why you bother with that miserable job" his mother often commented.

His chores completed he made his way to the kitchen and to his surprise sitting at the dinner table was a sight he hadn't seen for a while. Next to his mother sat his father smiling and looking as fresh as the morning breeze. Simon's mood lifted and although he was not one for emotional outbreaks a sense of gladness overwhelmed him as he took his place. However, he was also aware of his fathers fleeting visits and was cautious in his welcome he did not want the house he had built fall like a deck of cards.

"Alright da to what do we owe this privilege" doing his best to hide the enthusiasm.

"Oh I just thought I would come home and see how my family are doing. I hear you are making good progress, got yourself a steady job and are engaged to be married, excellent news I think"; before Simon could compose a response his father continued.

"I have a few appointments in town I have to take care of and want to spend some time at home and give some support to your mother".

"That's great news dad", he felt funny calling him dad it had been so long since he uttered those words, - "we have a lot to catch up on, I'll have to tell you about my job and you'll never guess who my boss, well so called boss is" the excitement now hard to disguise as he began to babble.

"Okay, okay, son there is plenty of time to reminisce we will talk after you have had your supper".

Bridget plated up his meal and her husband indicated that they should move into the next room laughing and joking as they went.

The importance of Roberts return was palpable to the return of the prodigal son. While it was true he had missed a lot of his sons emergence from adolescent to adulthood and the emotional frivolity connected with such a phase, he had Simon hoped time to make amends. He planned to make the most of his return but because of his fathers vagueness he was unaware of his stamina for staying home.

He finished his meal relaxed in his chair and scanned the room in which he sat, his eyes followed the contours of the form of the ceiling from corner to corner. It was not a solid square the lines sketching more of a large inverted L shape. The dinner table was large enough to accommodate six chairs, which were imprecisely placed around it. Along one wall interrupted by an average size two paned glass window frame which gave a view into an extra large back garden filled with flowers and shrubs planted by Bridget.

Numerous items of junk belonging to Simon and his brothers stole away hidden in long grass, which was abundant. Positioned below sat an old style Victorian sink large enough to bathe two maybe three babies at any one time, this was updated to modern standards. To the left of the drainage area of the basin was a small 2foot worktop,

beneath this stood the dish washer, an essential time saver for any housewife,

"an unnecessary luxury" thought Simon.

To the right a 6ft long worktop ran the length of the wall with storage space above and below, opposite there was more worktops and storage with a large integrated fridge freezer beside this stood a washing machine. This in turn led to the back door where the rubbish bin was situated, the floor tiled with pavement size stones creating the illusion of a bigger space.

After a lazy daydream Simon arose and continued his daily chores, doing the dishes wiping down the worktops finally mopping the floor. Bridget observed him in action commenting,

"there was a first for everything".

Making a pot of tea he sat down at the table and poured himself a cup and as he supped a sense of wellbeing descended on him as he smiled like a pleased plumber. He was soon joined by his father who sat at the table as if he had a purpose, Simon offered to pour him a cup when Robert enquired about something stronger.

"Yes I'm sure me ma has something hidden somewhere in the house" and fetched a bottle of red wine from behind the fridge, indicating a knowledge of her hidden cache.

He retrieved two glasses, not wine glasses, lemonade or maybe even glasses for consuming milk from. Cloudy marks covered them giving an appearance of uncleanness, however this was probably just down to lack of use.

Promptly sitting down Simon quickly relaxed to have a smouldering sup of vino with his dad. Few words were spoken at first just niceties and generalizations of the kitchen and its environs however after a couple of glasses the ice was broken and the lava started to flow.

"So tell me about your work son what does it involve" remarked Robert.

"To be honest dad it is absolutely horrible, I know it is a job and I would rather be employed than not, but it is really soul destroying; there is no job satisfaction, no anticipation of a different tomorrow. No constructive criticism, no lively banter with any of the other guys in fact every one just seems happy with their lot, a bunch of drones just following the leader without a dissenting voice to be heard".

"Well what took your into that line of employment" asked his father?

"As you know I never finished school and when I left without qualifications there was not many opportunities for unqualified school leavers. I thought this was the best of a bad lot when accepting the job. And anyways how was I supposed to live here and not contribute. I know mother would not expect anything but I would not take that kind of advantage".

"You know son if you don't like it move on, a job has to be enjoyed not endured. It is not a prison sentence nor is it compulsory or mandatory. You are young and there is plenty of work out there, it is just a matter of looking".

The wine flowed as did the conversation and the mood became more jovial as father and son talked about all manner of subjects. Simon enquired of his father of the history of his employment.

"well son my first employment was as a coal delivery man".

"Really a, a coalman" said an astonished Simon.

"yes I worked for old man Flint up on fossil mountain and I had to fill 25kg and 50kg bags full of coal by hand dug out from the side of the mountain. I then loaded a flat bed lorry with 50 sacks and delivered them over a 25 mile radius. I received 25p for each sack delivered and I worked nine-ten hours per day, six days a week, all before I met your mother you understand but yes that was my first job. A real dirty filthy experience, I mean at the end of every day I

was black with dirt and coal dust from head to toe. The dirt got into every nook and cranny, in the hair in the ears, up the nostrils, bjesus I almost had to have a steam cleaning every night and watch the blackness ooze from the pores on my skin, but in the end it was a job and you get used to the pitfalls".

Simon now slightly intoxicated began to stir uncomfortably in his chair and stared in his father's direction closing his left eye as he deemed this the cause of his double vision.

"So what about Hugh"?

"Hugh?, what about him" came the reply.

"Have you not heard from him?, I mean he comes here to supposedly help mother and to assist in the running of things, stays a couple of weeks and disappears as quickly again, that was some first impression, he was about as useful as a third wheel on a bike. What was his forte?" again petitioning him for an answer.

"I sometimes ask myself that question, he never was a very responsible person. But I thought his wit and charm might lighten the load around this place and anyways did he not play the guitar and banjo, two very useful instruments to learn" he replied with a smug grin.

"No I will tell you what he was good for, absolutely nothing. All he did was sit in that room all day and night smoking like a train, puffing like an engine strumming on that bloody banjo. He never attempted to help out, not only was mother looking after Roberta and me, he was like a long lost son, she cooked, she cleaned, oh' he was a nightmare. And on occasion when he could find it he would drink her secret stash never to replace it he was a bum and a waster".

Robert could see that his son was really worked up about the behaviour of his Uncle and was finding it hard to reconcile the actions of his own brother. He had no

explanation for his sudden disappearance assuming he had merely returned to his own home renovations complete.

"I had no idea he just upped and left", said Robert,

"Yes it makes you wonder what was he running from, a thief in the night fleeing a crime scene".

Simon now very animated left his chair and was standing in the middle of the room pointing and slobbering almost foaming at the mouth, but not quite. His father was old enough to realise that when the drink is in the wit flies out, In vino veritas.

"Do you want to know what your bastard of a brother did while he was here for that brief moment in time?".

His father sat in his chair stunned at his son's harsh language his violent tendencies bubbling beneath the surface. His pent up anger obvious as a volcano prepared to erupt. Simon had waited for years to rid himself of this burden, the silence he kept had almost took his short life and for a long time he had wanted to expose his vile uncle's secret. He had thought of visiting his father at his workplace and revealing all but held back in the belief no one would believe him, now in his presence his redemption was near.

"I will tell you what he did"

But before he could utter another word his mother entered the kitchen looked at her son and yelled, "Simon you drunken lout stop shouting at your father he is not well".

Hearing this Simon ceased in his outburst and returned to his chair.

"What do mean he is not well, in what way is he sick? he looks fine to me".

Bridget enquired of her husband if he had told him the news and when he replied no Simon again stood up and demanded to know what was going on.

"Your father has come home from working away all these years not as you may think for a fleeting visit but for a longer stay", his mother said softly.

An increasingly agitated Simon replied

"will you stop talking in riddles and tell me what is going on".

"Simon", his father said sternly I was at my doctor last month as I had pain in my abdomen. Tests were carried out and the results came back sooner than expected, initially the doctor informed me that it was a muscle strain but this has proved inconclusive. He came back with a more detailed prognosis and informed me that I have the big C".

"So, so, stuttered a confused son, that don't matter you can come home and be looked after by your family and we can do all the things we missed out on. We can go on a family holiday, you can teach me how to drive I can buy a car and we can go fishing, so many possibilities".

"I admire your optimism son I really do it is truly inspiring but lets see how things pan out. Now I have travelled a long way and I'm tired if you don't' mind I am off to bed".

Simon unaware of the profundity of the situation or of what he had just been told bid the two of them goodnight switched off the lights and climbed the stairs to bed himself. His room was airy with a slight breeze gently blowing in from the top portion of the two-part window which was that had been left ajar for the purpose of refreshing and clearing the dusties. Although drunk he wasn't in such a state so as to be oblivious to his actions, he drew back the bed clothes undressed and climbed on top of the bed wearing just the shirt and boxers he had changed into earlier. Reciting prayers from his younger years his mind was awash with a myriad of bloops and unconnected thoughts, and now I go to sleep per chance repeatedly swirled around in his head as he drifted off in a drunken sleep.

He had been asleep for a mere four hours when suddenly his eyes flickered open. "Christ I have to get ready for work", the utterance addressing no one. Quickly jumping out of bed, he felt a sharp pain in his forehead, which moved, steadily over his cranium resting at the back of his head just above his neck. There was nothing unusual about this pain as he had suffered it many times before in the form of a hangover. The pounding got worse as he searched but could not find a pair of socks as he rummaged through his sock drawer, finally opting for a pair of dress socks deemed sufficient for the purpose.

Out the door, rushing down stairs there was no reason for him to suppose anyone would be up at the time he goes to work. Running through the parlour to get to his shed he was startled to catch sight of his father sitting alone with just enough of the morning light breaking through the duskiness to reveal his presence.

" Dad, you almost give me a heart attack; what's wrong?", and not even bothering to wait for an answer he rushed on shouting as he went " what ever it is dad it will have to wait until I come home".

As he arrived at his designated work place, his hangover was in full swing, his head pulsated, feelings of nausea aroused deep within, and as he gazed at the pit he was to excavate, he thought to himself ,"no way today jose fucking death and dying would be preferable to climbing into that cesspit".

There was however, one bright thought floating and it made him smile through the pain and discomfort, it was the start of the weekend and tonight he and Lucy went out socializing. The restaurant already booked they would have a slap up meal before moving on to a nightclub for drinks, dancing and a touch of romance.

CHAPTER FOURTEEN

His routine completed he dressed in his favourite trousers put on the sassy shirt bought for him by Lucy, slapped on his 'Eau De Toilette' and made his way to her place.

Lucy lived a short distance from her budding beau and because he was early, normally he was late always keeping her waiting, he decided to walk and fill his lungs with fresh air as opposed to what he was used to on a daily basis. He thought about their future together and supposed that as his father was back on the scene giving him more time to spend with her he contemplated asking her to marry him.

"Why not?" he thought "I have been neglecting her lately maybe it is time I made an honest woman of her".

Happiness abounded him as he walked and thought of the two of them together. Suddenly doubt infiltrated,

"what if she says no, what if she says we're not ready for marriage, what if she declares me not ready?"

A single bead of sweat trickled down his brow as negativity attempted to take hold.

"No be positive!" he thought as he tried to shake the nonsense from his mind. "Why wouldn't she want to get married? Is it not what she has consistently asked about?" His nervousness made him tremble at the thought of her saying no and as he approached her front door doubting 'Thomas' and friends began to dissipate, gently fading from the process though simmering menacingly in the background.

She came out to meet him closing the door silently but firmly behind her; "unusual", thought Simon but never give it a second glance.

"Hi babe you are looking as wonderful as usual" the slipperiness apparent to all but him;

"we need to talk," she uttered,

"talk? Okay babe about what?".

Lucy began to speak and uttered just two words, "it's over!"

"What, what's over? He said the words almost choking him.

"Simon our relationship is finished' I want you to leave and never come back". She quickly turned on her heels stepped inside slamming the door behind her.

Agape, he stood staring at the door for several minutes wondering what had just happened before turning and walking away. Making his way to the lane, which leads out toward his home he came upon the remnants of a tree, the stump set back about two feet from the road in among the rushes and bushes. It had been an old one when completed but had been removed its offending branches over hanged and stooped dangerously onto the laneway. Its destruction unnecessary as removing the arm like branches would have sufficed, but progress and ever-increasing safety standards required it be taken out of existence as a cancerous tumour is exorcized from its unwilling recipient.

Sitting down his thoughts were drawn on the rejection just inflicted on him and he recalled how those young women felt when he himself ended an association he had had with them.

During his recovery, he had had the pleasure of the company of many a young flower but that was as far as it went. He was just happy to receive a kiss, a cuddle, and maybe the odd fumbling but he was not ready to settle down and go through the ritual. These young flowers however perceived such a union in a different light and assumed their first boyfriend would be their only boyfriend; such is the nature of their young unadulterated angelic minds.

The thoughts of which there were many clouded his brain and his thinking became erratic as he supposed to discover her problem or her problem with him. His resolve was resolute as he left his throne back in the direction of whence he came to demand answers. But who was he to demand anything, what if maybe she was having an off day. What if her time of the month was causing her excruciating pain that she did not want him to see her in such agony. Would not his returning and confrontation not escalate the situation.

Stopped in his tracks he held his head in his hands as he stewed on his next move. Indecision was palpable, his head was reasoning for him to go home and contact should be made the next day, his heart heavy with uncertainly as the green eyed demon introduced himself. Chances are she has met someone else and he was to be sidelined her coldness a definite indicator of subterfuge, again self doubt led him to deduct a what if scenario. What if there was someone else involved what was he to do about that, the intricacies and workings of the female heart are complicated and incomprehensible to the male thinking. If her heart was set on another what is to gained by intrusiveness?, there is no other choice than to let them pursue the dream of happiness. However, he decided that caution was the better part of valour and continued on down the lane toward home his hands stuffed firmly in his trouser pockets, his demeanour obviously dejected.

His mood was overly gloomy as he reached home and entering inside he cared not to make contact with anyone preferring to go straight to his room without recognition. He was acutely aware that solitude would only cause him to think of the disaster, which just occurred and thought to read a book of some sort, to focus his mind away in fantasy away from the realism of actual normal day to day activities. He reached for 'Thomas Hardy, 'The Mayor of

Casterbridge' and lay on top of his bed to read this great author's interpretation of the death of character. Although he had read it many times he knew the intricate reading would put his mind at rest helping him drift into a restful sleep.

Sometime later, after he obviously had fallen asleep he was awaken by his mother's calls. It was still early 10pm to be exact as he gathered his explicit thoughts and made his way down the landing and limped down the staircase rubbing the sleep from his eyes as he went. Making his way to the kitchen he entered and there sitting at the table was Bridget and Robert with looks of consternation on there faces. Pulling out a chair Simon sat down commenting why all the long faces as his mother poured him a cup of tea. He had no indication of the extent of the information relayed to him by his father, nor could he fathom the seriousness of what he was being told.

The lump in his father's abdomen had gotten bigger and he had to go into hospital the next day so doctors could ascertain the damage. This was not registering and when his father pointed out that it was a terminal disease and most of those afflicted with such a condition rarely survive, still it scored zero on the Richter scale. The concept just washed over his head, dying and leaving this world happened to other people not to him who had just came back into their lives after being away so long.

Bridget cried softly and quietly into a large handkerchief as Robert again admired his sons optimism but commented that it was

"misplaced and the situation was looking bleak".

He had obviously received devastating news but still could not convey it to his son; he tried to think of the perfect analogy or suitable metaphor to describe his illness and its consequences ergo enabling his son to understand.

"A rolling thunder echoed in the distance, a lighting strike indicated the spot where the young soldier fell, his body torn and twisted as the bullets left their fleshy wounds on exit. Transported in drape covered box, settling and resting deep beneath the permafrost never to see action again".

Jason deemed this a riddle and commented "why can you never speak straight, poetry is not one of my strong points, and I don't think it is appropriate for the occasion".

Exasperated with his sons lack of understanding Robert turned in his chair and gazed out of the kitchen window, only to ponder, what if?

A case for the defence could be built upon the fact that in all probability his son was otherwise preoccupied with matters only concerned to his own existence, thus his dereliction to the troubled interior of his father's predicament.

The business with Lucy continued with all the despair he choose to afford it, he carried on with his daily routine of going to work, coming home eating his dinner and retiring to his room to read. Each time the telephone rang his ears pricked up in anticipation, alas as awaays to no avail. He thought about her every second of every day counting the weeks as they slowly passed by even considering going to see her but a sense of pride always held him back, he had not yet lost his dignity; pride a dangerous and utterly futile attribute to possess.

Robert meanwhile whose condition had steadily deteriorated at an alarming rate had been given six months to live and was now confined to sleeping in a bed in the downstairs parlour having been sent home from hospital his tumour deemed inoperable.

Although this was not ideal and certainly not how Simon would have wanted to connect with his father it did give him the chance of spending some precious time conversing

and deliberating. Robert was afflicted with a malignant tumour whose aggressiveness was unmatched. The doctors and the cancer specialists had not come across such sarcoma. He was prescribed a batch of experimental drugs in the hope of combating the offending matter, however as this was an opening salvo the outcome was totally unexpected… an outcome no one predicted.

CHAPTER FIFTEEN

Eight weeks had passed from his last encounter with his beloved Lucy Ferrer and now his initial apprehension and fear had turned to anger. He was totally aware that she was not expected to come to him after the dissolution of their partnership, it was she after all who needed space to grow and find her own true meaning. But not even a phone call or a note or a message of some sort expressing solidarity for his troubles truly agitated him.

Simon still held true to the verse in the many poems he had read which summed up his feelings, uttered while liberating a white Dove; "if you love something release it from your grip, let it go, if it comes back it is yours, if it does not then it never was". These words, which he had seen in the poetry of Shelly, Byron or D.H Lawrence, had a true resonance to them if only for poetic licence. She obviously had her own agenda to pursue and Simon or his concerns were of little importance to her.

While he resented her absence admittedly he loved Lucy Ferrer and longed for her contact. Her beauty and demure qualities held a fascination deep within, he was afflicted with a yearning so desirous that it engulfed his every waking minute. The consummation of alcohol was a past time to be enjoyed occasionally, however, he thought to himself desperate times call for desperate measures. And settling down for a bout of unadulterated squalor hoping to lessen his pain; however as is always the case his problems still remained in sobriety.

Not only had he to contend with this situation, his father's condition worsened and a dark cloud hovered menacingly over the home. An ominous wind murmured throughout the branches and leaves of the trees dotted

around the landscape. He began to miss days off work preferring to buy alcohol and stand in darkened parts of the streets where the forlorn people gathered to share their woes and disappointments, blaming everyone else for their misfortune; little aware of or a failure to acknowledge the over used phrase 'God helps those who help themselves'.

Making his way home after one of his sessions he began to dread going any where near the house that had become a cold room for the living, secretly he was glad his beloved Lucy Ferrer no longer frequented his life. His father's illness had exposed the entire house to a concept hitherto unheard of, its unspeakable nature straight from the pages of 'hell' from Dante's Inferno.

The experimental drugs Robert had been taking in an attempt to defeat the onslaught of cancer had an adverse effect on his already ravaged person. It was heartbreaking for Simon to hear his father cry out in horrendous pain any time he attempted to move or adjust his frail body into a position of comfort while asleep.

On many of the occasions when Simon conferred with him he had learned that when his father was younger, eleven years old to be precise, he had had his appendix removed. A procedure carried out while under local anaesthetic where an incision approximately 5cm long is made in the groin area to remove a benign outgrowth on his lower intestine. This operation was successful and he carried on with life as normal.

The untried drugs had such an reaction that the offensive cells with no where to escape burst unceremoniously through his weakened abdomen and began to grow from his colon as a fungus grows from the stump of a dead tree. The scar was now a conduit for the cancer to mutate with a vengeance.

The entailing trauma resulted in a nurse visiting twice weekly to assist in the changing of the dressing and his own

GP calling once a week on a Friday to check his progress. Although Robert came from a Catholic background, his mother and father when they were alive, both having passed away twenty years earlier were devout and attended church methodically.

Over the years for one reason or another he had allowed his faith to lapse, however, he readily welcomed the local priest who would come and pray with him, redeeming his faith; also administering the sacrament for his salvation. And while the priest never preached, condemned or eulogized he sensed the evilness of his parishioner's affliction as the stench of death filled his lungs with repugnance. This unpleasantness permeated the house and its environs eventually seeping into the very fabric of its foundations. For his part Robert being at the centre of this obnoxiousness was totally unaware of the effect it was having on those around him.

Over time the district nurses became less frequent, one could only assume that they had had their fill of this desolate place, subsequently Robert resorted to changing the dressing himself. This not only gave him the impetus to try and break free from the restraints placed upon him it also gave him the chance to realise his mortality. He lived in hope for some miracle cure; his body may have been shattered his mind however was intact.

He was often prescribed mind numbing tranquillisers to dull and ease his pain, analgesics of an experimental nature were tried and tested on him, still he cried out in his sleep for just a modicum of relief. Occasionally he would ask for assistance in shaving, Simon would be the dutiful son and gather to gather his razor, an old fashion type that still required a blade changing as opposed to the actual razor; shaving cream, a small mirror large enough to see a decent reflection and a basin of hot water.

Bridget had in her desperation all but abandoned her husband, effectively turning to alcohol to numb her senses. She did not want to face up to her responsibilities nor did she want to lose the only thing that seemingly gave her a reason for living. She responded by leaving the family home and joining the 'forlorn' people leaving Simon to care for his father and his younger sibling. Shopping, cooking, cleaning generally replacing his mother as well as going to his own work. Any time she did return would only be when she had been drinking heavily where she would attempt to embrace her husband on his deathbed causing him excruciating pain. Her actions did irreparable damage to an all ready fragile situation. In effect she could not cope with the reality.

Simon looked at his father who was now a shadow of his former self, he had weighed at least fourteen stone for almost twenty years, now he was down to seven and was just skin and bone; the fragility of his arms necessitated Simon to shave him without request. This became routine and although Robert objected in the strongest terms he had to gave in to his son's pragmatism with a realisation it was for the best.

A most distressful aspect of this was the images inflicted on Simon as he worked with his father. Robert had to change his dressing on a daily basis and would often do so while food was being prepared, always requiring his sons assistance. Reluctantly, Simon would become a space invader, his senses assaulted from every angle. As he removed the soiled bandages Simon Sanders seen at first hand the 'BIG C', the cancerous growth emanating from his fathers lower abdomen. He thought of a cauliflower growing from out of the earth viewed through a time lapse camera, inching slowly as it broke through the soil to form perfectly shaped florets. This was covered in dried blood, freshly oozing blood and steam rising to fill the room with

the smell of rotting flesh. A most unpleasant and unsavoury experience.

This horribleness continued for two years, a situation untenable under any circumstances and during this time father and son would speak at length about the latter's life. Robert told his son about his childhood, about his early schooling, in the process he learned more about his grandparents.

Another link he was totally unaware of as both of Roberts parents had passed away six years before the notion of Simon was ever conceived. Granny Sanders he discovered was an angel who had been taken from this life through lung cancer. 'Granda Sanders', was described in less flattering terms; he was depicted as a little brute of a man with a heart of stone who mentally and physically abused his offspring. Simon was astounded by the story of his forebears and shocked at the level of brutality inflicted on his own children.

His grandfather who he knew very little about apparently was an enigma wrapped in a total contradiction; whenever he would go drinking and according to the story this was excessive, he was always the one in the corner spouting crap about how much he loved his wife and kids. Robert, however, painted a different picture revealing the truth about this vile man.

His grandfather, Charles Sanders, had married Sarah Goodie, they had eight children together four boys and three girls; another revelation for Simon. At first they appeared to be extremely happy but with eight children to care for the apathy soon set in. Charlie Sanders worked hard as a clerk in a local bookmakers but rarely provided for his family; this would be understandable if he had been putting money aside for the future of his kids, but this scenario was never on the cards. Any money he made was spent on the horses

and drinking down the pub where he professed to be a loving family man.

Simon learned of how when Charlie Sanders would spend his weeks wages in one day, losing them on duff horses and pissing the rest down the drain, he would then make his way stumbling home and expect his dinner to be waiting for him and when it wasn't there was hell to pay. This information troubled Simon as he enquired of his father,

"why would he behave in this manner if he did not contribute to the housekeeping?". Robert pointed out that this was his style, he totally dominated his wife all their married life, he got whatever he demanded no question.

"You have to remember son" his father would say almost in a whisper his vocal cords and voice box straining indicating the level of stress his frail body was enduring; "this was a time when women were expected to cater for their husbands every whim, they were to stand in the corner and never eyeball their self-styled masters".

"Huh, unlike the women today" uttered Simon unnoticeably. His father continued reminiscing of how his mother struggled, scrimped and saved in order to put food on the table. Robert was the eldest of four brothers and was more often than not spared the wrath of his wicked father who tended to focus his attention onto the younger boys. Seamus 17 years, Thomas 16 years and Hugh 15 years were taken out of school and put out to work by their father; thereby removing a burden from him and placing it firmly on the shoulders of his young charges.

It was thought Simon "a very traumatic upbringing". And when told of how to put a semblance of grub on the table Granny Sanders used to pawn her husbands best suit every week, his inner hilarity raged; it was not just the father's clothes but the brother's best duds were also fleeced. Seamus was by all accounts a real ladies man and

although forced into hard labour he did enjoy the benefits and independence a few silver coins afforded him. He managed to buy himself a suave new suit and a fine pair of brogues, which had a fair degree of mileage in them as all in the household wore them religiously. This attire was passed between the brothers and in turn was marked out for the pawn shop.

On more than one occasion when the pawn shop was neglected, the money needed for some other necessity, the clothes remained in bondage then all hell broke lose. Charlie Sanders would demand of his wife of about his finest and when told the inevitable the beast emerged and she was beaten to a pulp, and when he learned of the boys clothes suffering the same fate they were set upon with equal venom. "Yes it was all fun and games growing up", mused Robert, "which is why", he continued "I vowed to myself if ever I get married and have children there will self-determination all round, children are children and they deserve a childhood".

However, Robert most often described how his father who was after all his maker, how in his later years was struck down with cancer was bed ridden and often cried out in his sleep in heartbreaking agony, of how he struggled to come to terms with such a concept.

"Who would have imagined" sighed Robert as he continued to converse with his son.

He also revealed that he was a promising schoolboy soccer player and could have made it into the professional ranks, this had been cut short over a leg injury however. A small tumour had been removed from his lower shin thus ending his career leaving him with a slight unnoticeable limp. This was invaluable information as it gave him an insight into his fathers past, proving we are all frail human beings

A disturbing development arose where talks where taking place which excluded Simon. For over a year the doctors, nurses and clergy who where calling on Robert were advising, recommending, that he should retire to a Hospice for the terminally ill; a notion he vehemently resisted stating,

"Once I go in there I am never coming out of it again".

He was clinging on to the false hope offered by doctors of the possibility of a miracle cure.

The situation now as it stood was unbearable and they had to drive home the reality that there was to be no respite and if need be they would enforce the mental health act compelling him to enter the facility. After much debate and a lot of tears he agreed to their will.

The ending of a long drawn out nightmare for all concerned was upon them. There were no goodbyes, Simon went to work as usual in his morose state, returning much the same way.

As he entered the home he discovered his father gone; a weight the size of Mount Everest lifted from his shoulders, he walked into the kitchen and there was Billy sitting at the table tapping the top with his fingertips as if waiting for an answer to an unasked question.

"Where's dad?, I arrived earlier to an empty house expecting to see him, I have asked Roberta and she doesn't know. What is going on around this place"?. A tone of anger resonating in his voice.

Simon made a pot of tea, fetched two cups and sat down to explain and try to enlighten his older brother to the situation. William or Billy as he preferred was six years older than Simon, at 5"7 he was slightly taller than his younger sibling, he had a round flat face with a high brow, deep brown coloured eyes, intense and mysterious, a trait familiar in the Sanders boys; he carried not exactly a beer belly but an extended waist line. His mannerisms as far as

Simon concluded where similar to his long dead grandfather, cheeky and petulant. Billy was informed that his father must have been moved to the hospice and he was welcome to join his younger brother in visiting him. As usual Billy made his excuses adding he had to pick up his wife and run few errands but wished to be informed of any developments.

He continued to sit at the table as his brother exited and poured a refresher cup from the pot, as he did so he engaged the deafening silence with mute comfort that not only enveloped himself but what seemed like the whole world.

Gone was the hustle and bustle of strangers sitting about talking into their tea and coffee cups, making light unnecessary conversation, their falseness an abomination and wholly transparent. It did not strike him that his father was gone, he obviously did not see the significance but the death knell had been lifted, that pungent despicable stench had lessened in strength and potency with a fair deal of relief. The clouds that had appeared so prevalent and foreboding casting shadows above had dispersed into the ether.

"What now"? he anxiously thought, "without substance there is no meaning". The routine he had followed astutely and to the letter was now befuddled, there was no purpose, his equilibrium was off balance and he dithered, finally acquiescing to his inadequacy.

Walking into the small parlour that was formally his father's bedroom he listened intently to the uneasy silence, the space now clean and tidy. As his eyes moved slowly around he gazed forlornly at the inanimate objects still remaining. A small six foot by four foot bed stood alone except for a plastic chair with a large rubber ring attached, used by his father whenever he managed to leave the confines of the bed to give respite to the many sores covering his legs, back and buttocks. A bedside cabinet sat

opposite the chair, its single drawer slightly ajar, a further 5 inch crevice below the drawer was occupied by a small note book with various scribbling on its cover, crouching down in front of it he retrieved the curious looking pad. Opening it he began to read and was stunned by the contents.

The enormity of what he had found soon became apparent as he continued to read; in between the leaves were the thoughts of a dying man, an account of a journey set in a world of utter pain. Robert had unwittingly put pen to paper describing a desolate, despairing existence, intended only for his eyes. He explained his remorse for working away from home, even though he knew it was essentially a dereliction of duty, he was in a constant state of denial.   It was also a record of his hopes, fears, unhappy expectations and dreary ramblings. Joyous reminiscences of his youth portrayed a picture of carefree self-assurance but crucially and more importantly as far as Simon was concerned it contained a voice of how and why. His father's emotional struggle to understand the evil within was heartbreaking to read.

"Where did this come from and why has it descended on me", wrote his father. "Have I lived my life the wrong way? Have I offended someone unknowingly? what is to become of my family, my wife, my sons' and especially my beautiful daughter".

Simon could see the resignation as his father acquiesced to the cancer and likely death. The writings also recalled the search for a possible reason for the outbreak of this despicable disease;

"maybe I have consumed to much alcohol in my wanton abandon, neglected my wife once too often and this is my repayment. Perhaps I should have maintained my body more listened to its nuances, obeyed its commands - went to the toilet when instructed instead of holding it in and letting

it fester in the bladder things may have been different". The musings offered an insight to Roberts's mental state and revealed the frailty and mortality of someone considered an indestructible giant among men.

Simon approached 'Marie Byrd house' with a degree of hesitation its huge Victorian façade instilled a sense of dread in his already vulnerable perception. The building was set back from the main road in its own grounds surrounded by large swathes of greenery, grass, shrubs and small hawthorn bushes. It was located approximately 10 miles from his own home. Tall imposing oak, ash and yew trees stood in sporadic pitches through out the one acre sight their branches and leaves stretching to capture all available light.

Large bay windows adorned with plain net curtains faced out to give an impression of neatness. Large Iconic columns with scroll like volutes unfurling majestically decorated the front entrance of the house, with a greyish blackish door welcoming those who dared to tread. Familiar aromas lingering with the unmistakable odours of urine and unwashed carpets greeted him as he stepped inside - death and despair resided here.

A senior nurse, clerk, ushered him into a small office and attempted to explain the gravity of his father's position, her drawl straight from the hills and valleys of the country side.

"Your fathers condition worsened over the past couple of hours, are you aware of the situation?", but as she uttered the words and speaking at length all he seen was her mouth opening and her lips moving, however no voluble sound emerged.

This lack of recognition was more than likely down to the fact he didn't want another quasi-professional foretelling his fathers demise. Eventually released from her grasp he entered the room where Robert had been placed

and again he was faced with further traumatic scenes. As he lay on the bed which, considering its purpose seemed enormous he appeared as a newborn having just been placed in its cot after birth, a scene indicative of the wastefulness of this despicable affliction. Its effects on a person an abomination.

The doctors in their wisdom had administered morphine and its effects were now telling; he was in an induced coma and every breath he took threatened to be his last. The breathing appearing robotic with loud inhaling and exhaling intermittent with grunts and groans. Simon sat for five hours with his father witnessing this gut wrenching scene before leaving stunned and bemused to inform those of concern of the situation as well as to catch some respite.

It was four in the morning of the following day before Robert finally succumbed; however, he did regain consciousness long enough to say his goodbyes to Billy, David and a few other close relatives. He had been at the hospice for 12 hours his earlier prophetic words now predictive and frightening. His last words were to an apparition of his mother who he had seen sitting in the corner of his room, informing her he was fine and would be there soon.

The intensity of the situation was lost on Simon, although the death was expected the shock of his actual passing did not resonate with him. While there were quiet tears from Bridget and those closest to the occasion the realness of the loss and his apparent inability to surrender to its consequences indicated indifference. Although this could have been a mechanism for non-acceptance, people's perception vary greatly.

After the funeral a semblance of normality, which for so long had been missing from the Sanders household descended ubiquitously after all the coming and going that had taken place previously. The visitors and well wishers

ceased and the quietness and stillness proved unnerving but for Simon who half expected Robert to walk through the door at any minute smiling and laughing his usual laugh.

Another troubling factor for him occurred when his beloved Lucy Ferrer attended the funeral with her new beau.

"Hi" she said meekly and tried to introduce him as she offered her condolences,

"this is my new friend Robert" she hissed, the irony completely oblivious as she embarrassingly attempted to assuage her guilt. With absolutely no stomach for niceties and a complete and utter hatred for her he dismissed her out of hand and realised "now I am truly lone".

CHAPTER SIXTEEN

Six months had passed and events had moved on considerably. Bridget could not face life in that big old house alone and had decided to sell up preferring to go and live with her parents, who at sixty five were still relatively in good working order. Her mother welcomed her daughter readily. The old house was sold and selling everything apart from a few mementos of her life with Robert, she and Roberta moved on.

Simon too had moved on cautiously; gone was his self-indulgent pride and narrow mindedness, replaced with openness understanding and a theory that life was too short to be conceited. However afraid of making repeated mistakes he was acutely aware of the notion 'that too much of a good thing is bad for you and should be avoided, equally 'too much of a bad thing is soul destroying' and should be discarded at all costs. He was determined to get it right and went out of his way to avoid a déjà vu relationship.

He had moved into a self contained bed sit room in town located above a local shop. This consisted of a room with a double bed that for all intents and purposes doubled as a sofa, a lounge and writing space. One corner of the room was fashioned into a neat niche into which two large shelves were placed approximately 5foot and 8foot off the floor. A 20inch colour television sat precariously on the middle shelf seemingly its breadth an inch or two wider than was intended, an inoperable remote control sat on top.

Books from a previous tenant adorned the top shelf; titles included 'Buddhism a complete guide, Teach your self to speak Hinduism, notes included: and a History of everything unimportant' an obscure almanac by an equally

obscure author; various other leaflets and pamphlets of a religious nature were also neatly packed.

Opposite this and just beyond a large bricked up chimney breast stood a small gas bottled cooker with a crudely built shelf ajar, rickety and most unlikely to support anything placed on top. Two large windows facing out onto the backyard of what seemed a public house allowed a semblance of light into the dwelling and were adorned with curtains with flower patterns and reeds imprinted on them.

An obnoxious looking steel sink with a small drainage area perched worryingly against the freshly plastered wall, its beige colour indicating a misnomer. A small round mirror hung from an untimely nail inserted, cracking the plaster in the process. A miss-matched ceiling light with shade hung lopsidedly from the off centre of a ceiling fitted with fireproofed tiles. An off the cuff bare red coloured rug lay on the floor approximately 12 inches from the door and completed the furnishing. Not exactly a palace but a home from home, "some where to put his head" he mused.

Simon sat on the chez long and stared out through the curtains at the bleak scenery beyond, he suddenly felt nauseous as a flood of thoughts hitherto unknown crowded his mind. He stood up and paced the room stopping only to gaze at his reflection in the circle;

"I do look a shade pale" he gathered as a rumbling growled from his belly. Globules of sweat began to form on his brow and he suggested to himself that maybe he should lie down.

The invasion of his mind grew more intense as he lay on top of the bed, a picture of his so-called uncle HS appeared at his forehead. He felt a nasty occurrence rising in his gullet as he imagined HS and his gangrenous face smiling and slobbering as he poked and hauled at his person, he could taste and smell the lack of character, of the alcohol and the body odour. He watched as he heaved and humped

116

striving to fulfil his dastardly deed; his head started to throb and his brain pulsated as waves and waves of neurons appeared and disappeared. These repressed memories emerged with a vengeance, then curiously as quickly as they had begun they dissipated with equal haste.

Continuing to lie on the bed he stared at the tiles on the ceiling and considered the previous tenant must have been a heavy smoker, the tiles were stained with a tinge of brown and fawn colour. Larger circular stains with ring shape inserts indicated a leak from the roof or maybe a burst pipe he could not discern.

He counted the tiles which were approximately 24cm by 24cm in diameter, one, two, three, four, five, six, seven, eight ran the breadth, one, two, three, four, five, six, seven ran the length. The tiles appeared to be suspended on wires and snugly fitted strips of plastic, an intricate piece of illusion giving the impression of floating in mid air. An attack of conscious occurred as he continued to count, first there was HS now came the reminisce of Lamia although he often viewed her offence as an awakening; a sort of rite of passage, still, he was far too young for behaviour of such nature. He actually enjoyed their encounter when it happened, however it was out of place and he could see now he was ill-prepared for such contact.

Now as the essence of Lamia filled his nostrils its pleasant intimation a comfortable distraction from the disturbing memories he now termed jungle demons; his psyche was constantly pursued by thoughts of 'what if' and 'if only'. What would have been the outcome if he had tried to maintain a presence at Stephen Unlike's home all the those years ago? What if he'd hung around Lamia more just to feel her near him? Her touch and hirsute nakedness flashed sporadically across his injured mind. If only he had ignored Sammy Sercle when he had first seen him standing alone by the shop that morning on his way to school, a

second thought and a third thought jumped into his reasoning,

"I wouldn't have got involved with those other no-hopers stealing and missing school. He now agreed and understood when his father used to say that "those days were the best days of your life", now he was left with a plethora of question marks. He became a people watcher, a studier of workers going about their daily business, of the painter, the plumber, the skilled tradesman, "I can do that" he thought. But in his consciousness he realised he was never made aware of the importance of education in this game of life. Slow on the uptake Simon Sanders now fully appreciated the circle on which the world turns and of how he had missed the boat. Not because he was over intelligent, pompous or brash, none of these characteristics applied, too many obstacles had been placed in his path and his attention was directed elsewhere.

Lucy Ferrer crept into the mire, images of her smile flashed intermittently between the three. Hugh, Lamia, Lucy, "what a mix" thought he. Thinking of Lucy he concluded that their long term relationship had ended too abruptly, there was no explanation, no goodbyes, leaving far too many questions to mull over. Mixed with these laborious musings he started to contemplate the unthinkable, "would it not be better for all concerned if I were to leave this Godforsaken world? Supposing I were to die then this torture would be over and no one would have to listen to this inane dribble, especially himself".

This kind of philosophy went against every thing he believed in, he was taught in church to respect life and to cherish every waking day. His deliberations continued "all human life is precious and no one had the right to expire it except God, in who's eyes it was considered an eternal sin". This reflective mode allowed him to consider the concept of death and dying, while the idea of non-existence carried a

resounding fear, no one wants to expire before their time, he also understood we can't pick or choose, the notion and dread of dying began to wane. His fear subsided as he concluded "surely death was preferable to a non-specific life filled with everlasting worry". This realisation gradually dispelled the underlying terror of dying so prevalent in human society. More and more he wrestled with this dilemma finally drifting off to a restless sleep his mind weary and exhausted.

A number of days later when the melancholy finally lifted its ugly presence from his domain he decided to leave the safety of his new abode and venture out to enjoy if possible the fresh air that was in abundance all around him. In so doing it would give a chance to attempt to reconnect with the outside world thus ending his self imposed exile.

Descending the stairs he approached the door leading outward, pulling the curtains to one side he could see through the plate glass window that it appeared a wonderful day with a clear azure coloured sky above, with not a cloud to spoil. Taking deep breaths as he walked his lungs filled with the goodness of purity and feelings of well being abound providing a natural enthusiasm, something that had been lacking of late. As he walked past a small eatery named 'Henrys café' he happened to glance at the front window and was drawn inside by who he observed sitting at one of the tables at the large window.

Bridget Sanders sat alone and had he surmised been there for some time on account of the three empty coffee cups sitting patiently waiting to be retrieved by an incompetent waitress. Simon sat down moving the cups to the next table saying hello in a manner of not thinking what was going on around him.

"Ma what are you doing here?" he exclaimed "sitting by yourself, where is Roberta, more importantly how the hell are you?". Obviously animated by her presence and unable

to contain himself he continued "how are our Grandparents, I hope everything is well?".

He did not notice at first but Bridget was looking rather haggard and dejected and as she raised her slightly lowered head he could see she was in some sort of mess. He gazed upon those once perfect features that were once a shining light, and all that stared back at him were knotted eyes from gnarled, aged tree bark; the foliage of its branches wilted and withered. Her eyes while not having lost any of their lustre looked staring and wild, empty and alone; the large dark circles beneath them and her complexion adorned with deep gouges weathered and leathered. An old sofa adorning a second hand furniture shop floor a perfect resemblance.

"Is there a problem"? he asked, half knowing there was before she answered.

"Hello Simon" she replied her voice rasping and wheezing. "Everyone is just fine I just needed somewhere to gather my thoughts and get my bearings I'm not to sure about this place, I just needed to get away from the hustle and bustle of that house. And anyways I am no longer a teenager and it is not right that a married woman should go back and burden her parents".

Simon thought her comments strange, equally surmising she had had a fall out with his grandparents.

-"Ma" he went on to offer an opinion, "you could hardly be called married, a long suffering young woman who has been dealt cruel hand leaving her a widow would be more apt", ordering a fresh pot of tea as he pulled a chair from its resting place. Sitting down his concern grew as she began to cry,

-"wh-what is it ma, handing her a sincere paper handkerchief", the type which are placed on a table for use as a coaster.

"Your grandfather has been admitted to hospital with Leukaemia, he is in a coma and not expected to last the weekend" she blurted out matter of factly.

"Good grief" he thought "the cards are truly stacked against this family, we must have been cruel, evil bastards in a previous life, our come-uppance is sought with a vengeance",

"I, I didn't know he was ill offered he in a timid tone, come to think of it I can't remember the last time I laid eyes on the man", a conclusion he wished he never uttered. He looked at his mother's tear stained tired eyes and observed as they began to well, slowly the tears dribbled and began to follow a well worn route falling gently onto her saucer.

She went on to describe and explain his affliction and the impact it had on him, his wife and his brood adding quietly "no one knew he was ever ill such was the man". The grandfather was referred to as the 'quiet man' his taciturnity a trait to behold much like his passing, silent, dignified and without a fuss.

There was quite a large turn out for this patriarch both in terms of family and friends, a brave few travelled from England, Australia and America to witness the burial. Simon discovered uncles, aunts, cousins, second cousins, family he never knew existed; the surname 'Sanders' truly was global.

One aunt made a statement, which carried a resounding truth when she commented "that they would all have to meet in different circumstances and be jolly as opposed to the fact that recently the only time they got together was at death marches, weddings and funerals". And while a wedding was supposed to be a joyous occasion, for a majority of the Sanders clan divorce was a recurrent theme, such was the ambiguity of spouses.

After all the hustle and bustle of introductions to unknown family had died down and all had returned from

whence they came Bridget once again became fearful of the deafening silence she had the misfortune of experiencing previously.

The mountains of food provided by concerned family members and sincere well wishers filled all available space in the kitchen. The fridge freezer was packed with fresh vegetables, fresh home made vegetable soup, cartons and cartons of it. A wide selection of cold meats, cooked ham, boiled tongue, pork and tomato slices, salami, chorizo and a fine selection of cheeses took all the shelf space. Ready made sandwiches and an endless supply of milk weighed heavy on the mind. The cupboards had enough tea bags and coffee supported by copious amounts of biscuits, tea cakes, Victoria sponges and cherry and vanilla swirls. A grizzly bear would have been in its element upon seeing this Aladdin's cave at winter time.

Deciding what to do with such a bounty was a distraction for Bridget as she proposed it would soon become stale and moulded. She determined to donate most of it to a drop in centre for the most vulnerable. her mother was compliant apparently numbed at the realisation of losing her husband of forty years.

At the conclusion of her deliberation Simon learned that his mother had moved from her mothers house into a small apartment some ten miles away and had requested that "she look after Roberta for a couple of months". At least until she got back on her feet again when the sale of her own house was finalised then the two of them would be together.

This surprised and puzzled him as his thinking led him to surmise the last thing she needed was solitude after a bereavement as this only encourages an onslaught of demonic thoughts. He was also concerned about her drinking. Uttering quietly his inner thoughts concluded, "being on her own paved the way for bouts of uninterrupted binges although in reality there was not much he could do to

prevent it"; his inner anxiety voiced she was left to her own devices. The hubbub of the event dissipated and life returned to its former pace, however life for the Sanders had changed forever, the loss of such patriarchal figures proves a traumatic experience for all concerned none more so than those closely connected.

CHAPTER SEVENTEEN

Simon returned to his humble abode of new surroundings. Once inside he realised he detested the place, "this cannot be the final deal" he thought, its odd out of sync rickety furniture depressed him, the dankness of the decorum with its semi-blocked out light screaming out loud for redecoration. The smell lingering he could not discern its origin, charred burnt toast loitered with a hint of singed potato skins; intertwined and mingled, an overwhelming stench of stale beer and cigarette ends inched slowly upward from the yard beyond, finding an inlet through the window.

Among the fusty bedclothes piled beneath the sofa-bed lurked an offensiveness too revolting to acknowledge; out of sight out of mind he often thought, their squalid condition leaving a nauseous imprint on his already decaying senses.

He recalled his mother's house and the aromas of pleasantness that hung delectably from every nook and crevice, whether it was from her cooking or housekeeping it always had a refreshing character wafting from the rafters to the cellar.

Stephen unlike sprang forth and he remembered the bramble with their berry bushes and the Hawthorn whose clusters of flowers produced an earthy tang emanating a wholesome feel, the house always produced a freshly cut foliage flavour. He decided to air the room and promptly opened a window allowing a cascade of refreshed oxygen to flood in and returning the bed to sofa status sat down to gather his thoughts.

Suddenly he came face to face with Lamia who, dressed in a flimsy negligee eyed him desirously. Her tongue circled

124

behind her slightly parted lips as she slavered and drooled, running her hands over the semi-naked voluptuous body placed in front of him. Teasing and writhing she urged him forward grasping his hand and jerking it downward as he reached for her.

"Where have you been?", he cried, -"I have searched and searched for you to no avail, remember this was at your instigation and now I long for your touch". She then began to fade from view and as he called for her his voice echoing to a whisper he awoke with a creak in his neck the dream slipping from his grasp.

He began to feel uneasy about the whole sordid affair. His troubled mind now flooded with images of an unsavoury nature and he stood up started to pace the room in an attempt to shake the jungle demons. He was inundated with pictures of fishy doc striking him with the strap, the old man walking across the road pleading for him to stop, his spirit hovering above his lifeless body. The headless corpse of dickey McNoon hauntingly stalked him, its face a grotesque spectre of pain and horror as it spun through the cold night air.

Sitting down he broke into a cold sweat, his stomach contorted and contracted as he attempted to offload the offensiveness within. "If only this rotting bile would unleash itself from its shackles maybe I could rest easy" he murmured pleadingly to himself. After much effort he began to vomit, exalting at the sensation so much so he envisioned the lining of his belly had ripped clear from its sinewy tethers such was the force of his yelping.

As soon as he did he felt the heaviness that had descended with so much grief disengage, relax and gradually disappear as if it had just been imagined, unlike the gut wrenching-which was as plain as the nose on his face.

An unbearable thirst developed in his parched throat after all of this activity and he reached for one the few half litre glasses placed in the sparsely populated display cupboard. Standing at the sink he gulped down one, two, three full glasses of water effortlessly, salivating and drooling he felt the cool life preserving water slide over his murmuring glands quenching his dryness in a heartbeat. In a second breath he began to analyse and disassemble the thought processes occurring in his mind,

"what were these strange visions that seemed so life like almost as if they were actual?" he mused, "if they are dreams they appear realistic and familiar but I have no recollection of such events" he concluded with an air of suspicion. Simon was unaware of the power of grief and the impact trauma has on the senses, however, he continued to pick the bones of this carcass - searching - probing.

A prolonged knocking started on his door, the kind indicating a timid disposition as it appeared someone was looking to gain entrance.

Reaching for the key in the door the stillness and quietness of the room emphasised the action of the mechanism as the inner components of the mortise turned and unlocked. The latch released sliding backward into its bearings and the door with its creaky hinges opened and a slow mournful groan echoed into the hallway. Standing there before him was a young girl of about 16,17 or 18 years of age, he could not discern.

"Hello" he said with a radiant smile "and what can I do for you", he added with a welcoming voice regular and assured.

"Hi" she returned "you don't know me but my name is Selene Trully, I saw you at grandfathers' funeral, however you never acknowledged me", she concluded with an air of hesitancy, her lips quivered and voice stuttered as she spoke.

Taken aback at the obstinacy of her observation Simon quipped "I'm sorry I unintentionally injured you but who did you say you were? I know you say you were at the funeral but who are you, what is your ilk?". His annoyance clearly visible in his tone and posture.

"My mother is a second cousin of your mother and she and I travelled here from Canada for the burial. I know it is a bit strange just turning up at your door without proper introductions but no-one seems to know much about you".

"Oh so you are a relative, well why didn't you say that in the first place, my apologies for being so obtuse, come on in and have a seat and take the weight off" his mood and demeanour immediately improving. He eyed her as she entered the aroma of cheap scent wafting in behind her, all the while thinking "she was very attractive", as she sat down on the inexpensive people carrier.

"Let me take your coat and make yourself comfy, I'm sorry all I can offer you is a glass of milk", he said disappointedly. The young lady declined his offer scanning the small living space in her descent.

Selene Trully stood approximately five foot tall with her shoes on, and these shoes, which happened to be flat soled didn't really increase her size so she would have stood just under five foot bare, footed. Her hair was of a dirty blond colour and hung shower curtain like off her head, rolling slightly on to her shoulders inching down her back. She had a round petit shaped face with a small nose and green hazel coloured eyes, her stature was small and as he observed on the removal of her coat she was blessed with round plump breasts. She was of a pleasant disposition as he listened to her speak with a touch of gravel in her throat he thought "she had the voice of an angel". Not wanting to appear to formal or imposing he stood at the window as he asked her about herself.

"So you must be the daughter of 'Sophia' my mother's distant cousin, the one we thought was a figment of her imagination when she spoke of having relatives in America". She confirmed his assertion adding

"yes my mum and I are staying at the local hotel in the town centre we are flying home tomorrow, I just thought I would come and introduce myself and perhaps get to know you better, you are after all a relative, I don't know of any others".

"Oh really don't you have any in America?", replied Simon inquisitively.

"Well yes but mum has fallen out with most of them I am not sure why but you know older people always arguing over something trivial" she said with a heavy sigh, a response laboured with a hint of normal practice indicating it was just how adults behave. "You got that right", he cried, "adults can be very stupid and devious at times their pettiness an absurdity to behold". They both laughed in agreement of each other's views.

The laughter fizzled out and a comfortable silence descended in the room as he glanced out of the window at the clear blue sky with the sun beaming he uttered to himself "that light is hurting my eyes". Reaching for the flimsy curtains he pulled them across just so the fabric blocked the sunlight and faint shadows fell into the room. He stood with his back to her and murmured

"so how do you like Ireland?"

completing the task in hand. He turned almost 360 degrees to face her and observed her smiling as she replied

"I can't really tell from what I have seen but it seems fine, it also tends to rain a lot".

Simon noticed as she spoke that the top two buttons on her shirt like blouse had been meticulously undone revealing a hefty cleavage. This alarmed him and he felt an uneasiness stir within in. She arose from her sitting position

and slipping off her coat manoeuvred herself deftly in front of him, just as a snake slithers.

Standing inches from his face he could see a warm glow emanating, her aura lighting the small space in which she stood.

"Are you aware of the trust you evoke Simon Sanders?" she uttered, the croakiness of her velvety voice loitering with intent. Before he could answer she was on her knees undoing his trousers, loosening the remaining buttons on her blouse as she withdrew his member. Shocked and unprepared Simon Sanders stood dumfounded, he could tell this wasn't her first time as she licked and slurped, all the while purring, groaning and wheezing with pleasure.

Before long they had moved to sofa and not even bothering to unfold the mechanism releasing the bed they were on top of each other. When it was over she casually dressed herself and prepared to leave, "hold on a minute what just happened there?" he murmured in an angrily tone.

"Sorry babe gotta go, got a flight to catch but I will write to you", her nonchalance infuriatingly frustrating as if nothing had happened. He reached for one of the books, one which appeared heavy and threw it at the closing door; "huh what a brazen hussy he stressed, coming here and behaving as if she can do what she likes, messing with peoples emotions then casually disappearing. I have a good mind to go and tell her mother of her", he protested annoyingly to himself. It wasn't long before a rush of thoughts invaded his troubled self and after a period of a couple of hours and a tough negotiation session during which time nothing in his mind had resolved any outstanding issues he decided to confront his tormenter.

"But where is she staying"? his conscience strained and his brain ached. There are two local hotels in the vicinity, within walking distance.

This was another headache for him as he assented "how do I make contact?, what am I to do go to both hotels and ask does a Selene Trully and her mother have rooms booked in your hotel? they'll think I am off my head, a complete loony tune. And if I do happen to see her or her mother what am I to say to either? Excuse me Mrs Trully, you don't know me but you and my mother are related twice removed on your father's side, which makes me a kind of blood relative. Your daughter Selene arrived at my home earlier on the pretence of introducing herself as a grieving relation. I welcomed her into my home and before I knew it she seduced me".

"Who would believe that story"? And as he thought a little more about it he realised it did sound far fetched, so much so that he decided against revealing the sordid episode to anyone.

The following week was one of tortuous anarchy, his mind mangled as he struggled to come to terms with the event of his second cousin twice removed. She had entered his realm and he had succumbed to her evilness.

An irascible desire for self harm lurked in his psyche as the jungle demons formatted an idea hitherto kept in check by the voices of reason and correctness. However this new plan, which had been touched upon briefly by long forgotten voices, was vociferously adamant in its appeals in that they were suggesting new and destructive methods of ending ones existence. This was enhanced further with the knowledge gained from his mother that she was indeed a mere fifteen years of age; "mature for her age gesticulated Bridget",

"in more ways than you think" thought he.

But where did a fifteen year old acquire knowledge of such a mature and adult nature? She has obviously been active sexually he observed when she performed fellatio on him without much encouragement. This perplexed and

irritated him as his thoughts descended into a chaotic mire of uncertainly; what urged this girl to act so casually and reckless?. It had not occurred to him before but he now recognised and acknowledged that in his short time living he had experienced enough trauma for multitude of people. He also realised that if such behaviour ever surfaced then he would be blamed for leading a minor astray. This was a serious criminal offence, unlawful carnal knowledge punishable with a prison sentence. No matter who instigated it or who took the lead she was a minor and he would be held accountable.

The jungle demons were now having a field day and an assault on his conscience was underway. As this emotional blitzkrieg peppered and infiltrated he began to panic; soon he was starting to agree with the ogres of the forest.

Maybe it would be better for all concerned if I just got it over with, if I were to end it all now then at least my torment would come to an end. He deliberated on different methods of taking his own life but most of these were distasteful and through his minds eye most of them involved to much of what looked like pain. Like using a rope to dangle from the rafters or from some unfortunate banister, however, there seemed to be too much planning required for this approach. Too many things could go wrong. What if he changed his mind mid way through the process? Dangling freely from a rope does not provide much room for manoeuvre when you decide your are better off living.

The cutting of the wrists with a sharp instrument. Again the image conjured up of slicing the skin and the red colour of blood oozing slowly from a gaping wound astounded his psyche, it sounded in his head like a painful experience. No, he wanted something simple, which by implication suggested a cry for help. This too however evoked images of a cry-baby, a wailer who was just looking attention because he's had a bad stroke of luck. And even though his

fear of dying had eased he still thought it better if he continued to live. Although it has to be said his life experience thus far was far from imaginary it could not be denied whatever spin was put on it.

All of this thinking and in effect what was mere claptrap moved him to feel nauseous, a pale white descended upon his strained features, he appeared to have aged in an instant. There were flecks of grey mingling in his thick black hair, a feature he was renown for, dark circles loomed large under his eyes. Crows feet marked out a weathered and fawn appearance. His tortuousness continued for a lengthy period and no matter how he tried he could not escape its foulness and while his long term memory was still in absentia, his short term memory was conjuring images of unknown origin.

Flashbacks of sexual depravity occurring on persons unrecognisable poured through his mind; acts between males occurred where behaviour of such was frowned upon by decent society. These were intermittent with visions of death, of headless corpses, of bodies laying in coffins, the life drained leaving only a shell. Realising it was futile to try and block out the visions he attempted to read a book, his thinking, distraction better than reflection.

CHAPTER EIGHTEEN

Opening the hard back cover of the obscure title 'Buddhism a complete guide' he could not help feeling a new venture was underway, one, which was probably meaningless. Although he had heard of the term 'Buddhist' he had no concept of it's substance, it's basis or ideals. However, undeterred he began to read and as he realised the principals of the book and it's doctrine he became aware suddenly of the problems reading such literature could pose. Even though it was just a guide outlining briefly the ethical properties of the Buddhist thinking he just could not get his head around the existential theories the book proposed.

He was of the opinion and did agree with the theory of the individuals' right to self-determination and also where one was responsible for his or her own actions, he felt the idea of death and reincarnation was way over his head.

This concept while new to him provided an insight to his limited thinking, a factor most likely brought about by his limited schooling. This indication of a lack of education proved his narrow-mindedness.

The Buddhist's also suggest meditation as a way of discovering the inner self, a deep analytical rout of ones processes of thought. Of crystal clear thinking where one supposedly discovers true meaning to the conundrum of life. In the right frame of mind this may be so but Simon Sanders was not in that place and had not been for a long time. He continued to read and found himself fascinated with the theory contained within this until recently unknown concept, that is, unknown to him, however, Buddhist teaching had been in existence for centuries. This was another thing to add to his unending to do list.

The stillness of the room rebounded as he pondered the writings of the book, his demeanour improved as he soaked up the comfortable silence now engulfing his living space.

Frequently and most annoyingly this was interrupted by the hustle and bustle of the activity beneath him something he had not recognised before. Muffled voices could be heard along with strange noises similar to that of what he could only describe as cash registers being operated. He could distinguish the unmistakable ca-ching of buttons being pressed as the tote up for goods purchased was sub-totalled. And the ringing and whining of the till receipt as it chucked on its cogs, struggling to force its way through the thin slice of an opening before being unceremoniously ripped from its base and presented to the often perplexed customer with his or her change.

 He could also hear the rumblings of other machines in operation, a loud whirring noise climbing and climbing akin to that of a steam boiler as it achieved its boiling point finally reaching a crescendo and falling into a dense thud, he could not imagine the origin of this.

The unambiguous sound of a telephone was instantly recognisable. Although not of the new ring tone type of beeps and dots but the old style constant ringing of bells. As he contemplated he realised that this must be the hub of the community, a place for locals to gather, buy some unnecessary groceries and generally chit-chat. Suddenly there was a loud knocking on his door, which shattered the tranquillity and interrupted his musings.

The rhythmic rap rap rap rap, pause, rap rap indicated to Simon it was serious or something important and with apprehension in his gait he approached and opened the door. Standing there with a paddy cap on his head was this peculiar looking man, unrecognisable to Simon, chewing the cud or what looked like a lump of turf. Shades of green

and dark brown grunge were caked around his mouth with spits of saliva dripping onto the stubble on his chin.

Introducing himself as Ivan Koniving and speaking with a twang of countrified oaf he informed the now even more nervous Simon that "the wife had sent him to fetch him as there was a phone call for him downstairs",

"Oh, ok thank you for the message," replied he "I'll be right down". He could hear the inner rumblings of Ivan under his breath as he turned to go back down the stairs;

"Does she damn well think I have nothing better to do than run up and down stairs after her tenants? I have my own work to do and it won't be done any quicker with this charade", his voice gradually becoming fainter as he descended deeper.

Simon paced the room in deep thought, "Who was calling? More importantly who has his number?" "Who did he give it out to?" He could not recall; he then realised he had not give his number to anyone, he had no number to give as he did not have a phone, he was of the opinion no news is good news. Leaving the room, he ventured down to answer the call.

The phone was situated at the back of the shop next to a door used only by the landlord for access upstairs, however to reach it he had to enter the shop as normal paying customers would do and negotiate some heavy duty obstacles otherwise he would just leave by the front door. A deep chest fridge freezer, a stand up sliding door fridge containing lemonades, milk, butter and other dairy products, all strategically placed to provide a niche for the pay phone, which was bolted to the back wall.

"Hello" he answered placing the receiver to his ear and as the voice on the other end replied; a loud whirling startled him, whining noise coming from directly behind him. Turning almost 360' degrees he watched as a woman wearing an apron stood in front of a coffee machine holding

a small silver jug under a nozzle. At once, he instantly recognised the cappuccino maker and the loud noise was the steam heating the milk in the jug, the same sound he had heard in his room but could not recognise. "Huh there is a time and a place for that" thought he silently but made a mental note as he was partial to the odd frothy coffee.

"Hello, hello" the voice on the other end said frantically "Simon are you there its me your mother can you hear me? That boy is in a world of his own" she thought.

"Yes hullo ma I can hear you I was distracted by an accident in the shop there", obviously making it up as he went along. "What is it and how did you get this number?" he was ignorant of the fact it was a public phone and the number was available from any of the numerous directories; all she had to do was inform the operator of the name of the shop.

"That is a lovely way to speak to your mother" she replied, "what is it!", "I'll give you what is it". Hearing an obvious tone of irritation he apologised profusely, "I'm sorry ma I have a lot of things on my mind it was just a slip of the tongue" says he unconvincingly.

"Just to let you know a letter has arrived here for you, it has been sitting here for a week but how would you know when you never call to see your own mother the one who gave birth to you", her despair and annoyance apparent. After more profound apologies and promises of regular visits, he informed her he would be around later in the day to collect his mail.

As she continued to speak about absolutely nothing he took the phone from his ear and watched the earpiece. Seeing the words she was uttering in miniature drifting from the piece and hover around and about his head although he could not hear them.

He began to resent the notion of having told more lies to her, he had no intention of ever calling on her. He just could

not face or stomach seeing her drinking her life away and he knew she was drinking again as news had reached him quietly and without much fuss of her regular trips to a local off-licence. Any such meeting would only lead to a shouting match where even more hurtful words would have been advanced on each of them. However he resolved for common decency and more importantly to collect his mail, to make a flying visit.

Hanging up the phone he turned to be faced by an obstacle course in the form of a mountain of cartons. Large boxes containing all sorts of produce were being placed in a line at the back of the shop in preparation for storing. While he was on the phone a delivery of goods for the shop arrived and was being unloaded; He had to negotiate a giant slalom to get to the front of the shop. As he twisted and turned he came upon the coffee machine and promptly asked the woman behind the counter for one of her specialties. Small talk dispensed with he retreated upstairs to enjoy his frothy milky coffee.

Simon decided to take the bus to his ma's. The journey lasted approximately 35-40 minutes and it would give him time for reflection, also it was more than likely that this mode of transport would go by the scenic route whereby allowing him to view the wide open country side and possibly provide inspiration for a topic of conversation, something different from the norm.

Surprisingly the coach was full of people their destination unknown he did however manage to position himself at a window seat in order to serve it's purpose of stirring the grey matter. The journey began and he, eyeballing no one stared at the open landscape beyond, his gaze was drawn toward the wildlife carrying on its daily routine watching as the birds flew nonchalantly to and fro. The animals of the farming kind stood around in their pastures masticating profusely, the occasional heifer making

a mess in its perambulation, oblivious to the obvious fate that awaits it. Fixing his gaze toward the grey sky, which appeared to be enveloped in a blanket of coloured cloud of charcoal and dismal grey his thoughts clambered in a tumbling fashion as he tried to focus on the reason for taking such a trip.

In a daydream trance his mind was awash with a plethora of nondescript images. One particular image out of focus struggled through the mire to the front. The sight of this made him instantly feel nauseous and a cold sweat developed within. A grinning face of HS appeared with its eyes transfixed upon him; he tried but was unable to shake himself from his reverie. It seemed no matter how hard he tried the image grew more intense and now Simon felt a great fear enclosing around him. Constricted and shackled he pictured himself tied to a bed his arms against the headboard, he struggled to fix his eyes through the mist on the ties that bound him.

Turning his gaze toward his trembling body his legs as heavy as lead were position wide apart. Through the darkness and the mist at the foot of the bed the convoluted figure of HS appeared with menace. His heart raced and pulsated the blood pumped and quickened; he could hear the throbbing as loud as a base drum. Seemingly with no escape from this intrusion he began to scream at the top of his voice but nothing could be heard, no sound emanated from his mouth, a waking nightmare. He was taken out of his daze as the bus came to a stuttering halt and he imagined all the passengers were staring and aware of his peculiar encounter. However it appeared it was just the end of the line and he and whatever passengers where left got of the bus. "Phew" he murmured to himself "so much for the scenic route" and continued on toward his mothers flat.

He tried not to dwell on what he had just experienced but he did conclude that when ever his family or relatives came

into focus unwanted memories emerge, .however this was just a recent observation and supposedly it is only natural to blame others for his misfortune. The truth of the matter is he was unsure who was responsible for his mixed up mind if not himself.

Entering his mothers flat his apprehension was evident in his nervous glances around the small abode. He had not seen her in a while and did not know what to expect.

"Come on in" she enthused, "how was your journey? I know that road can be a bit rough at the best of times what with all those humps and bumps".

"Oh it was just fine, I didn't think it would be that long, that bus seemed to stop at every stop" he grumbled lethargically, "I know but there is no express bus for such a short trip" she offered with a hint of empathy. "Well no matter you are here now sit down while I make a pot of tea", she indicated to a spot on a small sofa and left the room.

Sitting down he looked around the tiny living space she now occupied although it was small it was still bigger than his was. It was neat and tidy, no television to be seen, however there was a small unit with a cassette/radio on top situated were a TV would have stood. There were a number of ordinary pictures hanging from the wall, a lamp standing in one corner and a small shelf supporting a vase of fresh flowers. The room was airy with a bouquet of lavender hovering and he surmised with a touch of uncertainly she had got her life back on track. Bridget returned with a large tray containing a teapot, cups and a whopping great plate of sandwiches of chicken and ham, a side plate with an array of biscuits was also evident. "This is no indication you could do with a good feed but you are looking a bit pale and gaunt, you need to keep your strength up" she observed as any concerned mother would. -"Don't start" he murmured quietly as she poured him a big mug of tea.

They conversed on a myriad of topics and also reminisced about better times when her husband and his father was alive. Simon ascertained that he hadn't many memories of his dad growing up what with him away working and all that while his mother remarked that he was too young to recall the holidays they all had together as a family, adding as a side thought, his reckless rebellious mode had almost cost him his life".

"That accident caused you brain damage it was only because you were so young that you survived at all" added she with a hint of cynicism. Simon was acutely aware of his actions and the damage inflicted,

"But am I to apologise forever for growing up?" he added with obvious scorn. "You don't know how it was to grow up without a father, no one there to look up to or to idolise. He was not there to set an example or to keep check whenever I stepped out of line and you, you had your own problems, I could not follow your lead. I probably would have ended up wearing long hair and earrings if you had have had your way. And what about Roberta have you seen her lately?"

Bridget sat cross-legged and tried to keep her composure during her son's tirade. "Well have you seen my sister or visited her or called her? I'm sure she misses her mother even though she had abandoned her". Bridget was scathing in her retort, she may have been a slight woman but her bite was still venomous.

"Listen young man for your information, yes I have, she stayed with me over the weekend, and she is fine. She has gone back to her nannies' as that is what she prefers; we both spoke about it and for her best interests that is the way it is going to be".

Simon stared straight ahead as his mother finished her outburst, silence descended as gently falling snow and he went into deep thought. "I've done it now, like always I've

gone too far". A picture developed in his mind where his mother slapped his face continuously and he begged for mercy and forgiveness. The scene repeated on a loop as he withdrew into a limpet shell. He did not notice as his mother left the room and continued to beat himself up. "Oh my God what have I done, I rarely see her and when I do I'm nothing but obnoxious to her, I don't deserve to be alive or deserve to have a mother there is something wrong with my fucking head", he began to sob furiously.

****

It may appear to some that he overreacted to this situation but one has to be aware of the fragility of this young mans conscious mind. He has suffered trauma from a young age and what may seem trivial to the average person was in effect a major dilemma to Simon Sanders. This simple quarrel with Bridget had the potential of jettisoning any progress in his recuperation deep into the unknown, affectively setting him back years.

****

He sat with his head in his hands trying to figure out his next move. Drying his eyes with the sleeves of his Sunday best sweater, which he had put on especially for his mother he lifted his heavy head and looked around the room. The ambience first felt when he arrived disappeared and was replaced with a forlorn hope, the same he had experienced so many times before.

CHAPTER NINETEEN

His mother returned and tossed an envelope in his direction, "here" said she "this is what you have came for you might as well have it" and she returned to her seat.

"Thank you ma" he murmured almost silently almost begrudgingly. "You are more than welcome" she cried, as he looked and caught a faint smile on her face. Scrutinizing the postmark he realised it had an overseas stamp on it, puzzled he began to wonder where it had came from. Whom did he know in England? On the back of the envelope there was a printed return address, which he studied for a long time; Stead's Hotel and Country club Albury, Tiring, Hertfordshire England.

Finally after a number minutes it could not be defined how long as he talked and thought at the same time, he asked of his mother, "hey ma when did you say this arrived, I can't really make out the post mark the date is all smudged". "Oh one day last week I'm not sure which" offered his mother. What Bridget neglected to add was that she did not know when the letter arrived as it had at first been posted into the communal post box situated in the hallway of her apartment block. She had by chance noticed a pile of unopened mail on top and recognised her son's name. It could have been sitting undisturbed for weeks if not months as Bridget readily conceded she never checks it. With a shrug of his shoulders Simon ripped open the envelope careful not to tear the contents, the paper inside was headed with the Hotels name and logo at the top right hand corner of the single sheet letter.

'Dear Mr Sanders, Further to your application for the position of porter/handyman I am pleased to inform you we

can offer you employment with our company. It is a 24 hour on call position and requires that you live on site. Accommodation in the form of a room in staff quarters is provided rent-free. Payment of wages is on a weekly basis and you are required to work one week in arrears. Please telephone the number above for confirmation of receipt of offer and acceptance/or refusal of position. Sincerely N. Farlington, general manager'.

He sat staring at the page in his hand almost in a daydream, his eyes would have pierced the sheet had not Bridget intervened.

"What's wrong son you look as if you have seen a ghost"? "Is it bad news"?

"No mother as a matter of fact it is good news, very good news but for the life of me I can't recall applying for this job".

"Oh is that all a job offer? I thought it was something important like a cash fall or a stroke of good fortune although I have to say that's a rarity in this family".

"What!" he snapped, like a red flag to a bull, he raged "is that all? Not important, do not be so disingenuous, this gives me a chance to get away from this backwater. To make something of myself it gives me a chance to gain some self-respect and earn myself a living. Typical of you mother condescending and critical, well I'm accepting I'm sure you'll be glad to hear and if I go I won't be coming back".

Then just as he was about to continue with his rant about how badly put upon he felt and of how the deck was stacked against him a flash appeared in his head and he was stopped mid sentence.

An image of himself with his father manifested in his mind having a conversation about work and his progress. The image was clear he could hear him saying,

"You might as well go it will be an experience and if you don't like it you can always return".

His father was talking from his sick bed as Simon appeared holding a paper, a job searcher, it was then that he began to remember. He had seen the job advertised in a local bulletin and was considering applying for it but because it was in England a distant land, he had misgivings.

"That was over a year ago" he pondered. "God that had slipped from my mind what with all that has happened".

His reflections carried a hint of sadness as he fell into a semi melancholic state, he wanted to glance in the grubby mirror but feared the pale sickly reflection he might have looked upon.

The loss of his father really began to invigorate his senses, although it had been a year since his demise Simon without realisation had numbed himself, had blocked the grieving process from his psyche almost as if the episode never happened. And now that he needed advice and counsel and reassurance the pain pierced deep, "typical" he assessed "never there when you need them".

Simon slowly came around from his musings and decided he had said enough to his long-suffering mother, without uttering another word he left silently without glancing back.

CHAPTER TWENTY

Back in the despairing living space he called home he sat on the frumpy sofa and considered his next move. Looking and scanning his belongings he dwelt on the characterless features attached to their drab existence.

"My father was right, what is keeping me here?". "Surely there must be better out there, a life more fulfilling; removing the pamphlet from the envelope of the job offer he gazed at the photographs highlighting the luxurious, marvellous surroundings at Stead's Hotel and Country club.

It was an old country house dating back to the earlier part of the eighteenth century and was set in it's own 5 acre plot of land. The house had changed ownership a number of times over the preceding decades and was now converted into a 36 bed roomed upmarket hotel. It had its own silver service restaurant and bar, also adjoining were tennis courts, a nine hole golf course and a large outdoor swimming pool. Inside was a fully equipped gymnasium with all the latest fitness machines available. Patrons could also avail of massage rooms to gently caress and nibble tired limbs after a hard day's workout. The photographs included a large dining room with individually placed dining tables adorned with white cloth bishop mitre napkins. The type seen in all of the plush restaurants around the world in a different era. Constructed, formed and manipulated into a shape resembling a bishop's hat by waiters and waitresses with too much time on their artistic hands.

Also prominent were crimson coloured table cloths draped over the 2-3-4-6 place settings. Expensive solid silver cutlery stood out with their gleam. The walls featured reddish brown wallpaper with red satin curtains hanging

from two large bay windows tied back their pleats forming perfect origami.

Away from this setting advancing first through the reception and into an exotic lounge area, the main feature appeared to be a fantastic log fire with a marble hearth surround. Wicker baskets filled with chopped logs sat opposite each other on either side of the marble; a large mirror with an intricate gilded designed edging hung directly above giving a real homely feel.

Several dark coloured elegant doors presumably of walnut or mahogany indicated further rooms leading from the lounge. "Very impressive" thought Simon lifting his eyes and gazing through smudged dirty windows of his flat; "anywhere was better than this place".

As his dreamy state slowly left his muddled mind a melancholy descended to stifle and congeal his thinking. Flashbacks of a convoluted nature trickled as water flows over protruding rocks; images of events of the past grew more intense and he began to feel nauseous. " I'm not sitting here going through this again" shaking his head as if to jumble the unwanted memories forcing them into the bowels of the hypothalamus, the section of the brain that processes and stores memories. He hurriedly put his coat on and quickly left the room and as he stammered down the stairs he thought about a cool relaxing walk in the early evening air.

Walking down the hallway passing through a door onto a small porch that lead outside Simon could see that indeed it was a pleasant evening and as he passed the front of the shop he could see a commotion of some sort occurring inside. Not wanting to appear nosy a fleeting glance was all that was forthcoming from him and he sauntered on his way. Although in some regard inquisitiveness and concern can be misconstrued as prying and intrusiveness by certain sections.

To the casual observer who might have happened to have seen Simon out strolling around on that particular evening an impression of nonchalance and congeniality would not have been a wrong assumption. This unremarkable young man walked slowly but with an air of confidence, his hands inserted deeply into his front trouser pockets appeared to be lost in thought. At times he would whistle some obscure tune and gaze at the dark night trying to name the stars floating in the cosmos, a picture of subdued smugness you might think. However nothing could be further from the truth for this young mans mind was wrecked with guilt and confusion. Visions of Lamia with her Goddess like body and aroma of freshly scented flowers flooded in behind his eyes, the intensity was such that he could actually taste her sweetness and could smell her as he passed by a bed of roses planted in some unknown flower patch, these images made him feel a gladness to be alive.

It was not quite dark in fact almost a duskiness had descended to give an in between feeling and he could still make out some of the birds that resided in the small wooded area adjacent the road which ran to the next village. Purgatory

Simon had often seen men and women, couples and others out walking their dogs beside this unofficial beauty spot; it appeared to be a place where the canine friends went to relieve themselves, to sniff and roll about, picking up each others scent before unconcernedly sauntering on their way. Large blackbirds hovered menacingly above the trees, ravens or crows he could not discern not even by the hoarseness coming from their gravely cries. A solitary magpie distinctive with it's white breast, soot coloured wings and nape landed, hopped around in the long grass as if searching for lost booty. Simon wary of the significance bid the bird hello, enquired of it's brother as a sense of

foreboding entered his thinking, however this logic quickly disappeared and he continued on his journey.

After a while, an hour or so he decided to return to the place that was causing him to distress and face the music with his jungle demons, but as usual the walk had the desired affect as a peaceful serenity draped his shoulders. Approaching he never noticed anything untoward either outside the hallway to his residence or occurring inside the shop apart from the normal activity attached to a small busy community meeting place.

Without much fuss he managed to slip unnoticed through the entrance. Although his mood had risen from its gloom and sorry state he still felt an uneasiness lingering as he closed his front door behind him. Removing his coat he leant over and switched on a small radio, which was tuned to a classic station, which he listened to from time to time, in between flashbacks and unsavoury memories.

He was not a lover of classical music nor did he fashion himself an expert on the great composers. He was aware though that this type of music tended to invoke a calmness and silent reverie in his psyche. One such composer he really enjoyed was 'Giacomo Puchinni' an Italian whose haunting musical compositions often sent a shiver down his spine, equally it would take him soaring with eagles. Whenever they were played on the radio usually in an Italian operatic tongue he would listen intently to try and learn the name of a particular piece, more often than not he would miss it. One he did manage to catch though was titled 'O Mio Babino', this included a solo by an equally unknown soprano whose memorable, evocative voice and lyrics simply reduced one to tears, melting even the hardest of hearts. As he turned the dial fine tuning the station he heard a simple knock on his door, opening it with no particular concern he was taken back to see Father Isfortune standing there before him. Unaware of the significance of

such a visitor he cheerfully enquired "yes father what can I do for you?".

The priest remained passive and unemotional retaining a blank expression as he spoke.

"Hello young sir I must say I have not been aware of your presence at church recently; is your name Simon, Simon sanders, son of Bridget Sanders? I don't mean to cause alarm but might we speak for a few moments?".

"Jes, father that's two questions without reply but if you must then come on in" and invited the priest inside.

The priest never commented on the flat but did admit as an after thought it was not unlike his own humble surroundings in the parochial house. "How do you do my son, my name is Father Michael Isfortune". "Yes Father Isfortune' I'm aware of you, how can I help?".

"Well my son I'll not beat about the bush and bore you with small talk, I am of the opinion that if you have something to say just say it".

Simon liked the style of this priest who unlike other priests he had the misfortune of encountering, those who would ramble continuously without ever making a point. Who would give half baked opinions on the irrelevancies of existence condemning those who dared to question. Father Isfortune told it straight and cut the bullshit.

"Bridget Sanders was on a bus today heading city bound when she collapsed onto the central aisle. Other passengers thought she had fainted and rushed to her assistance, after a number of minutes an ambulance was called and she was taken to hospital, here she died without regaining consciousness. It was over in a matter of minutes apparently she never felt a thing. She was unknown to anybody who was there and according to the police a quick rummage through her possessions came up with your name and this address. So my son the question is"?

A vacant look appeared on the young mans face. He sat staring directly at the priest though not actually looking at him his gaze transfixed to a spot on the wall behind him and tried to ingest what he had just been told. "Is this for real? Surely this is some sort of sick joke!" he murmured, the nervousness in his voice apparent in the shakiness of the words;

"This can't be happening again I mean it has just been over a year since father had died barely fifty years of age and you are telling me my mother has passed away. For God's sake she was only forty four, forty five years old, what a travesty".

"Are you sure she was called Bridget Sanders? I, I mean mistakes can be made it wouldn't be the first time". He began to get all flustered and was finding it hard to string two sentences together, he began further sinking into a traumatic melancholy as Father Isfortune tried to console and reassure him. The last thing he heard the priest mumble was something about "It being Gods will and that the lord works in mysterious ways".

As he spoke Simon looked and watched the priest as he appeared to drift away, almost trance like, first the body of the man vanished leaving only a small representation of a head hovering in mid air. It looked as if the head was imitating talking but no words or sound could be heard. And as he thought of what the priest had testified he felt a rage build leaving an overwhelming feeling of frustration at those inappropriate words. His emotions now were in a state of dispersal and when he tried to put things in perspective he questioned what sort of God would allow his so called children to suffer? What could he hope to gain in the demise of a patriarch and a matriarch whose folly was that they simply existed.

He now began to understand the meaning of Samara as taught in Buddhist thinking ; a process where in a societal

world the possession of all things material is discarded in favour of a search for enlightenment. In essence to envisage a route where the trials and often coarse tribulations of everyday existence are expelled in favour of clear thought, a distancing oneself from suffering of illness and death. The ultimate goal of the Buddhist is not to worship any 'God', for they bow down to no-one - their search is for Sunyata... emptiness that is empty of it's own emptiness; no beginning no end.

A rather bizarre theory and totally alien to the catholic faith but in the light of recent events Simon Sanders began to question not only his but the existence of humanity and all that had gone before. He acquiesced to the theory that a disbelief in God led to a disbelief in his only son Jesus Christ - in effect a discarding of Christianity - without this and all that this credo entails you have nothing; without this faith, the belief in a higher omnipotent spirit or presence, emptiness is realised. Also there was recognition that a religious belief of whatever kind brought order and contentment to otherwise chaotic existence and was essential in moral and decent society.

His mind now was awash with a surplus of different emotions; what was to become of his sister? How would she react to this? Roberta was a mere fifteen years old when she lost her father, now just over a year later her precious mother had left her for good, the despair was obvious. These concerns were eased when he learned that Roberta's situation would remain the same, she would continue living with her Grandmother for the foreseeable future. And while he may have had reservations about her well being he need not have bothered as his sister appeared headstrong over the whole affair, it was almost as if she like him had become detached from the gravity of the whole messy business as he discovered when they spoke at the funeral.

The service itself was a low key event with just a turn out of close family and a few unrecognisable friends of Bridget - some of who Simon and his sister never thought of as knowing their mother. There were no eulogies or long winded goodbyes as had happened at their fathers, just a simple service for the deceased and a quick interment in the same plot as the man she had married all those years before.

"How are you and how is everything at Grannies, are you settling in ok?" he asked all the while not trying to sound to morose and mournful. "Oh I'm fine, do you like my t-shirt?",

"A surprising response" thought her brother "she obviously has found a way to block this all out and maybe that is not a bad thing" he concluded with a shrug of his shoulders.

"Well as long as you are ok" and they both moved on to speaking about some other trivialities of unrelated importance.

In the grand scheme of things it appeared that Simon and Roberta had become immune to the sadness of grief. Yes they were sad but not on a level or with the same intensity as was the case with their father. It was almost as if an expectation had been realised as certainly Simon was aware of his mothers resumed drinking, his sister was also conscious of Bridget's unfortunate bad habit. However as in most cases of denial the questioning was frowned upon to be replaced with a policy of reasoning as to why.

Brother and sister had become less jovial and both had an exterior of seriousness shrouded on their young shoulders it looked as if the fun of life's great unexpectedness had been expelled, replaced with the constancy of melancholy. Simon told his sister of his intent to go to England were there was a job waiting for him and of how if he did go there was little chance of returning. Roberta's indifference was evident in her response as she

calmly told her brother to "go and enjoy his new life, don't be worrying about me I'll be alright at me nannies". Simon detected the tone of condescension in her young but maturing manner but decided to ignore it, the last thing he wanted was to alienate the only family he had left.

CHAPTER TWENTY ONE

The journey back to his bed-sit was full of doubt and indecision. On the one hand he dreaded going back to that wretched abode while at the same time his mind was in turmoil over his impending flight to a new life. In his deliberations he discovered there were more 'yeah,s than there were 'nays'; why shouldn't he go there was nothing keeping him in Belfast, his sister was fine and his brothers, well, his brothers done their own thing. He had lost contact with his older siblings and realised that they could in his absence cater for any needs their sister had. With this in mind he conquered his indecision and decided to forge ahead on a new venture. However...

His preparations were gliding along smoothly and he was busily tying up any loose ends still lingering. He had packed his one and only suitcase a relic from a bygone era that had belonged to his mother, as he recalled from a story she told when he was younger. She had taken it on her first holiday without her parents when she was sixteen; and while it was over thirty years old it was still sturdy, practical and fit for its intended purpose.

Next on his list was informing his landlady of his intention to quit her squalid lodgings, although this sentiment was not to be voiced, merely thought of, this was going to be a scenario he was going to relish. Not only was it going to please him no-end but the deposit he had paid (so long ago now it seems) would go toward his aeroplane tickets; one month down with a further one month in advance, an extortionate amount considering the location but he was about to be £400 better off.

He walked slowly, nonchalantly into the shop with determination abound, there were a few people milling

about busily doing nothing. Then he saw her, a picture of
beauty standing at the fresh cream and pastries counter.
'Venus de Milo' in all her glory and when she spoke her
voice was that of an angel. Standing agape, "who is that?",
he muttered under his breath and made a bee line to the
place where she was; trying not to appear over keen he
picked up two donuts with a healthy helping of fresh cream
smeared on them and promptly stood in line.

She approached the counter to pay for her purchase he
overheard the assistant as she greeted her customer.

"Hello Miss Donna Euryale", saying her name as a term
of endearment, "how have you been? We haven't had the
pleasure of your company in here for a while".

"Oh just fine I have not been out lately too busy
studying" she replied in a matter of fact way.

"And the folks, how are mum and dad?"

"Yeah they are pretty much the same, mother is still
working away on her milk round while father is toiling
away with his writing".

In normal circumstances Simon would quickly become
irritated at the level of interaction and mindless gossip but
on this occasion he sensed an opportunity and prepared to
stand in line patiently all the while listening to the laborious
conversation.

Small talk ended Donna Euryale paid for her goods and
prepared to leave the shop stopping to glance at the
woman's weekly magazines on the shelves before the exit
doors. Making his way toward her Simon accidentally and
smoothly on purpose nudged her gently as he tried to pass,

"Oh I'm terribly sorry excuse me"

She turned to gaze at him with an annoyed expression
and as both their eyes met he could feel the blood racing
through his veins like a transfusion. The palms of his hands
drew a cold sweat and a shingle reverberated along his

spine; he was not used to speaking to goddesses as he stuttered and fumbled ad infinitum.

To his surprise she introduced herself, which dispelled any perception he may have carried of her as being unapproachable

"Hi I'm Donna"

That is all... three little words of greeting but three little words that had such a profound effect.

"Oh hello" he uttered, the feebleness not unlike that of a ten year old who had just been asked for directions to some remote location. As the two of them stood in silence looking at one another the second hand of a distant wall clock, tick, tock, tick, tock at the back of the shop could be heard clearly, racing, racing as if it was in a hurry to reach an unknown destination producing an awkward yet comfortable silence.

"So how are you, and why haven't I seen you before?",

He murmured in a cheesy manner; before he could settle into a hackneyed smugness she replied with an air of authority,

"Oh I'm good and I could ask you the same question".

Realising that this could go on forever his aloofness relented and he quietly introduced himself.

"Oh yeah you're the guy who lives above the shop, so tell me how do you find it, living on top of all of the comings and goings of the day? It must be frustrating listening to that racket on a daily basis".

"Huh, I barely hear it" he could hear the condescension in his tone and in an attempt to relieve the tension added quickly

"I don't have to go too far if I'm short on milk or teabags or anything like that", an awkward wry grin struggled from his mouth. Simon soon began to feel the situation slipping away from him, he could sense the apathy by her posture but he didn't care to move too fast lest he scare the bjesus

out of her, he was experienced enough through past failings to admit nothing frightens a girl more than an over zealous approach.

He had done the hardest part with his initial contact but his thoughts still harked back to Lucy Ferrer as a profound pessimism began to creep into his psyche, and with this a shit load of unwanted jungle demons started to stir. If he hadn't have shaken them off he would have ended up losing any chance he might have had with Donna Euryale; with this thought he asserted that the past is the past and belongs in the past, nothing can be gained by raking over old coals.

They carried on with their small talk and when as slinky as slinky can be he had asked and she accepted, they arranged to go out for a coffee the following day.

"I think I'll have an early night tonight", he thought to himself; and as he rummaged around his tiny abode looking for nothing in particular he had nothing but happy thoughts. Preparing to retire Simon Sanders mood appeared upbeat and carefree, none of the usual demon thoughts that would plague his equilibrium were apparent, he had no explanation for this nor did he care. After a restful sleep the first he had in many a long night he awoke early next morning to the singing of larks as rays of bright sunshine shone through his windows. He had never recognised these before although they were probably always there, he had been too wrapped up in dealing with inhabitants of the jungle raging through his mind to notice.

Whistling and humming he got himself ready for the day and sitting down to breakfast he could foresee happier times ahead. After a quick self grooming, realising he was bereft of a mirror relying instead on the opaque shadow of his likeness on a stained window to reconstruct his usual dishevelled appearance.

"For goodness sake, I'll have to get myself a mirror, this simply won't do", he mused to himself as he tried to flatten the hair on the front of his head that resembled a cows lick.

On his way out the door he took out the letter he had written to his landlady stating his intentions to quit and looking at the brown envelope he slipped into a short reverie. "I don't think I'll be needing this now, if everything works out with this young lady there'll be no need to go anywhere". This may have been an admirable sentiment for Simon Sanders, however after one meeting with this young lady he was prepared to forego his plans for a fresh start. It was apparent he had learned nothing from the old adage 'once bitten twice shy'. Approaching the coffee house they were to meet, a sense of elation enveloped him as his heart started to race. "What the hell is this" he uttered quietly as a hot sensation crept through his pores, stopping to compose himself before entering he gazed through the large window just to make sure she was there.

She was, sitting at the very table he had unexpectedly met his mother at a year previously. He stumbled literally through the door and as he did an ominous foreboding was sensed and his warmth was replaced with a cold chill; ignoring this and brushing the feeling off as nerves he joined his female companion.

They sat for hours talking, chatting about one another although Simon as it turned out was listening more than talking, not because he had nothing to say, no this little lady was a talk - a - lot. He learned quite a lot about her, her family, discovering in the process she was an only child. She tended to speak a lot about her parents and her grandparents adding in her soft seductive voice

"Why have you never seen me before"?

Before he could answer she was off again talking about the stars the clouds the heavens and the ether. In spite of this Simon felt as ease in her presence and in view of all

that had went before he felt he could connect with her on the same level. After this initial first meeting they agreed to meet again at the same time same place and from coffee it swiftly moved onto dinner dates, the ball was rolling.

Simon Sanders had a new and invigorating purpose in life almost as if it was his first time of being in love when the thought of being with someone sends a ticklish sensation along the spine and the butterflies churn so much in your stomach that you almost feel physically ill. They appeared to be the perfect match although these were not his sentiments alone if he had learned anything from his past experiences he had gathered enough wit to gauge the women's feelings.

Everything was running smoothly as their relationship developed and blossomed, they were constant companions and done everything together then as they were out in one of their favourite restaurants celebrating a sixth month anniversary of being together she dropped a bombshell something he definitely was not prepared for.

"Simon I love you and I'm pretty sure you feel the same way",

At this point she was interrupted in mid flight as the starters of their meal was served. A sense of dread filled his bones as he prepared for the worst, a whirlwind of dire emotions permeated his mind and he could feel his mouth dry up as if he had just been served a plate of chalk. He thought of counter acting her pronouncement of intending split by proclaiming that he wanted a break just so that he would not be made to look a fool again. But as he tried to speak the words got stuck in a lump in his throat so much so it was almost as if he had pushed a clenched fist into his mouth.

The brief interruption over she continued,

"I love you and hope you feel the same and because we share the same feelings I was thinking Simon Sanders that the time is right for us to move in together".

After a quick splurt and an uneasy cough when he nearly choked on the lump in his throat a sense of relief carried with a deep apprehension descended on him.

"Wha wha what?",

He offered, stammering meekly, realising quickly that his first fears of intending doom and gloom were unfounded.

"I thought you had something else in mind Donna Euryale but hey yes why not, lets move in together, we are practically living in each others pockets as it is". Had Simon Sanders been fortunate enough to foresee the future he would not have been so quick to agree to such a foolhardy idea but hindsight is a great tool after the fact; it enables us to reflect on our fallacies teaching us thus. After a period of adjustment when all the essential parts were in place in preparation for the big move Simon Sanders had one more cog to oil in order for things to fit together nicely. It had been arranged for him to visit Donna's parents who had invited him to dinner as is customary for any budding son-in-law and also more importantly to introduce himself, after all he was the man who in all possibilities was going to steal away their only daughter.

The introductions were brief as they all sat down to a meal of boiled beef and cabbage served with potatoes mashed with creamed horseradish with the smallest amount of milk applied; "an unusual concoction but hey what the hell everyone to their own" thought Simon Sanders.

Gordon Euryale, Donna's father an unremarkable sort appeared to be a hard working man and worked early mornings at a farmers market sorting the fruit and vegetables setting them in stalls ready for sale. His speciality seemed to be potatoes as this was all he cared to

talk about; the size of potatoes, the weight of potatoes and the price of potatoes, "potatoes coming out of his ears", came silently under Simon Sanders breath. The mother Echinda Euryale was less active and did not work because of a mystery medical condition; she was overweight and thought nothing of constantly criticizing her long suffering husband. Because of this Gordon would leave for work at 05.00 and finish at two o clock in the day and tended to go straight bed to whenever his shift finished only arising when his wife retired, such was the vicious circle.

"So tell me son what is your forte? What line of work are you in and how do you intend to provide for my daughter"?

Gordon inquired of Simon as they both sat out in the back garden where they went to smoke a cigarette after what Simon thought was a long and arduous meal. The young man gazed at Gordon and watched in fascination as he put a cigarette to his mouth and took long forceful drags of smoke into his body and down his throat. Watching someone else do this with a cigarette always seemed appealing and virulent, the truth however was far less glamorous as he knew to his cost, _"once you start this disgusting habit it is virtually near impossible to give up".

"Well I'm hoping to get a promotion at work which entails a pay rise then we will see what happens after that"; this was a blatant lie as he was on the verge of quitting his job and fleeing to another country to find work but hey Gordon didn't need to have that knowledge.

"And when I have enough money together the deposit goes down on a house where we will live and get married one day, but that's all in the future we are just going to enjoy each others company for a while". "Commendable my son" replied his potential father-in-law- this hackneyed phrase really irritated Simon's bones and actually made his flesh crawl with embarrassment.

"But I think you are missing the bigger picture, it is bad enough that she is going to live with you, but at seventeen years of age she is way to young for marriage".

Simon stood up quickly as did the hairs on the back of his neck, almost ready for a fight with some ogre somewhere in the forest;

"But she told me she was twenty two a year younger than me and if she has lied about her age what else has she lied about"?

He felt an instant betrayal, a hotness together with a cold chill started to emanate from his pores as a nauseating feeling stirred in his belly,

"I think I'm going to be sick" he cried and rushed to the bottom of the garden, actually a back wall some six feet away.

"God you took that bad" said Gordon "how will you feel when you find out she only turned seventeen six months ago" he continued, laughing derisively as if he had attained victory in some glorious battle.

The implications of these revelations were really unsettling as they were already sexually active, Simon knew the danger he was in, however it maybe perceived by others. Technically she was under age and he had committed unlawful Carnal knowledge against a minor, an offence punishable with prison.

Simon stood with his head against the wall as the laughter resonated around the small enclosed space. The betrayal was intensely shattering on a level with what his so-called uncle had subjected him to in his younger days. Vicious images began to percolate his conscious like lightening rods racing across a dark cloudy sky in a violent storm. Grotesque visions appeared in his minds eye; the headless corpse of Dicky Nolan, arms stretched out as if appealing for help haunted him while the unmistakable voice of Sammy Sercle whispered "why didn't you sclow

down slcon" repeatedly, slowly fading into nothingness on the dark abyssal plain.

Simon Sanders struggled to compose himself and as the black reverie slowly withdrew his sight began to clear, he looked around the tiny garden and saw a picture of hatred in Gordon's expression as he sat in his deck chair with a dry wry grin on his face, enjoying his smug existence. "I have to get out of here" accented Simon as he ran up the garden pulling his coat from the branch of the small rose bush where Donna's father had placed it. Again and as he had done so many times before he fled the scene without saying a word to anyone.

CHAPTER TWENTY TWO

Back in his tired abode he packed his old suitcase furiously and reflected on the knowledge he had just gained. "Slow down think about this and consider your next move, rushing about like a headless chicken is not going to make the situation disappear, in fact it will only cause you to fluster and make mistakes", he uttered to himself in a philosophical aside.

He could have digressed and blamed Lucy Ferrer who had caused him to be in this situation in the first place or he could have blamed Donna Euryale who had blatantly deceived him, his mind was awash with a plethora of discontented thoughts. In the end he concluded that it was women's nature to lie and deceive especially to men who worship them. He watched intently as his mind swept back to thoughts of Lamia Unlike who had first introduced him to the ways of women both as objects of intense desire and the capriciousness of flawed character; this also demonstrated the naivety of his own character.

The business affairs with his landlady complete he was on the next flight to Hertfordshire, England, where a new and exciting phase on his journey he hoped was about to begin;

"This is it, no going back now", he mused as the aircraft took off into the horizon. Settling in his seat for the short flight to his new life of employment, the trip across the sea was a matter of 40 minutes, his feelings were a mixture of nervous apprehension and gladness to be leaving a place that was a cause of much of his misery, even though it was his home. He also had a curious sensation of regret over his departure. Staring out the small aeroplane window at the clouds below his inner voice toyed with his emotions; one

voice became many as their collective chattering urged him to stay at home, others compelled him, for the sake of his sanity to get the hell out of there. It was as though he was being informed that he needed to return his work was unfinished, however, he was unaware of this particular inference and dismissed the ramblings as nerves.

Simon Sanders was met at the airport by one of the secretary's of Stead's Hotel, an amicable looking woman plump in appearance and aged in her late thirties to early forties.

"Hello I'm Sandra, most people call me Sandy you must be Simon" she enquired with a smile.

For his part Simon who had never been on a aeroplane before and was not used to or aware of the affects of flying, where changes in atmospheric pressure can and often do alter the human body's sensory perception; hopelessly gazed back with a look of complete bewilderment. The rise and fall of air pressure had caused his ears to pop sending his stability out of sync producing in the process a wild sense of paranoia.

Feelings of being constantly scrutinized by people of every shape and size overwhelmed and constricted his thoughts,

"Who are these people and why are they looking at me", chipped away at his conscience. Sandra all the while was lost in conversation as she enquired of him about his history, "what brings you over here? Where have you worked before?

What star sign are you"? Although the relevance of this question was even lost on Sandra. Eventually when she failed to get any sort of response because of Simon's imaginary mental block she shrugged her shoulders and commented with a hint of scorn.

"Suit yourself then" and continued to lead him to their transport to the hotel.

His condition alleviated within about fifteen minutes, however, his perception deemed it a lot longer - when he tried to communicate with Sandra he got what he had expected, the cold shoulder. This had not bothered him before, he was used to the dismissive nature of the opposite- but on this occasion he became fully aware of first impressions having a lasting affect on co-workers, even potential friends.

It was about an hours drive to the hotel, it took a half hour of that to get out of London, the housing estates and city blocks seemed to go on for ever. Reaching the open country side the roads tended to narrow to lanes used solely for farmers and their tractors, their animals and slurry tanks. As he and his non-speaking host travelled along at what seemed a snails pace a sense of déjà vu emanated within his reverie; gazing at the open fields with their long swathes of green and wheat coloured grasses gently swaying in the wind. He pictured a flock of starlings swirling and turning in kidney and plough formations in the evening sky.

He wound down his window to partake of some oxygen and immediately his senses were quickly assaulted from all angles. A strong stench of manure, horse or cow dung, mixed with fresh air infiltrated the atmosphere, and instead of quickly retracting his window he took deep breaths of the offending odour; the smell evoking memories of his earlier infractions. In an instant he was back home again racing along the mountain roads as he and his friends laughed and joked, struggling as they did to ascertain the origin of such offences.

"That's them dirty stinking farmers", Sammy Sercle would say, "They would shite anywhere".

"No it is not ya bloody fool, it's the abattoir with all those dead animals", dickey Nolan uttered through the laughter.

"What?, I thought it was the smell of a skunk", offered Simon Sanders.

Smiling, looking out the window his gaze was transfixed at the broad horizon as he thought of happier times; intertwined with these came the jungle demons with their horrible images of death and destruction. Of his friends' lifeless bodies as their limp torsos floated and levitated in some sort of purgatory for the uncalled, their excruciating wails unnerving him. A cold chill descended along his spine and a shiver crept through his flesh. A fear gripped him and he began to perspire profusely - the smiling face of HS appeared at the front of his forehead as the globules slowly trickled into his tortured eyes.

"My God", thought Simon Sanders, "there is no escaping this, my tormentors are stalking me, what have I to do to put an end to this?". Slowly his trance withdrew as Sandy began to utter that they were almost at their destination; in his reverie the volume of her voice gradually increasing as someone turns the dials on the radio.

Stead's hotel, which was not visible from the road because of the large oak and elm trees that were wide spread throughout, their branches and leaves, masked any notion that a property was in the vicinity, lay at the end of a narrow lane that snaked its way python like through the trees. The trees formed a guard of honour as each one stood to attention along the route, their branches forking out in all directions almost in a deliberate attempt to hide the light. Emerging at the end the magnificent country house came into view its beauty and splendour a sight to behold.

Although Simon had seen the hotel in the brochure - actual reality was far more impressive; it appeared larger and far grander than any brochure could depict, the colours of green grass and brown bark refreshing and pleasing on the senses. The exterior of the hotel was painted in taupe and manila, its many window frames touched up with a

glossy white making the whole structure stand out perfectly in its green surroundings.

Simon stepped out of the car, instantly the purity of the air invaded his lungs invoking feelings of happiness and belonging; "perfect", thought he "this place would repair even the most wounded of hearts". Sandra or Sandy as she insisted on, led him to the front reception where Nikki Farlinton the general manager greeted him on his arrival. "You won't get much out of this one", murmured Sandy in a dry sarcastic tone and promptly waddled away about her business.

"Take no notice of her" accented Nikki in her cockney London manner, "nothing seems to please her", the emphasis on her style placed solely on articulating, the G in ing; as in thinG: -"she is havinG one of her off days she is not usually that rude".

The general manager was an attractive brunette aged about twenty eight years of age, small in stature and wore spectacles that highlighted her piercing blue eyes. She was immaculate in her dress and wore a fine pleated skirt with matching coat and necktie for the purpose of her status. Softly spoken with an air of authority she made a curious impression on Simon. After a quick tour where she told him of the aims and responsibilities of the hotel, she directed him to his accommodation. A single room in an accommodation block at the back of the hotel, next to the horse stables; fit for servants.

"Perfect" he enthused, "just like in the brochure", a hint of derision hid in his approval.

"So we shall see you bright and early in the morning for the breakfast shift 7.am until 9.am", said Miss Farlington as she preferred to be called, "welcome to the team Simon I shall see you tomorrow, get yourself a good nights rest".

His nominated room was at the end of a long corridor of rooms right next to what appeared to be an exit door, there

were approximately five doors presumably leading to other rooms and a toilet/shower room at the opposite end. His allocated room was small and self-contained with a single bed accompanied with a bedside cabinet, on top, which set a house telephone and a notebook. A medium sized window, which gave an uninviting view of a stable yard, was a centrepiece of the room; two drab curtains hung fluttering in the wind from the slightly opened pane. A large antique oak wardrobe complete with coat hangers stood in one corner and bare wood flooring completed the furnishing.

Simon entered and sat on the bed setting his unopened tattered suitcase on the floor beside him; almost at once the fustiness nearly overwhelmed him, the smell unmistakable as it was the same stuffy mouldy odour possessed by unlived in places. Opening the window further he felt the new breeze drift in and surround him, in doing so the stench of the stable yard hitched a ride. Wet damp hay, manure and the sound of horses neighing and stomping their hoofs against the stable wall as if striking out in protest at the harsh conditions in which they had to exist emanated loudly.

He watched with interest as the five horses came trotting up the pathway with their charge hands in the saddle;

"What's this?" he thought to himself,

"It doesn't mention this in the brochure, horses, stables and aromas of the animal kind, I don't think I care for this".

At once he felt a pang of homesickness and wanted to flee,

"What have I let myself in for" said he as he closed the window and sat down on the bed. Thoughts of his father invaded his conscience,

"I wish he could be here for consul" he sighed despairingly, a reassuring word, a pat on the back was all he longed for.

His apprehension grew when he heard voices outside the accommodation block, distant at first but gradually getting closer as they made their way up the stairs. Simon began to feel uneasy, an uncomfortable warmth accompanied with nervous tension flooded his veins; he had felt this feeling before - in the company of strangers and he suddenly became aware of such outside his door. Sitting on the bed a nauseating illness stirred within,

"What is this"?, I thought these notions were a thing of the past, something left behind in the old world", he murmured grotesquely,

achingly, quietly under his breath.

His inner turmoil was disrupted by a gentle knocking on his door quickly he stood up and tried to compose himself, shaking off the damn dark reverie that had enwrapped his psyche. He opened the door slightly and peered agonisingly out of the small allowed crack, as he did so he witnessed a vision of beauty in the guise of a blonde haired young lady.

Not wanting to come across as someone weird he opened the door further and with a welcoming smile he managed to splutter,

"hello", from his by now slightly drooling mouth.

"Oh hello", she replied, "you must be Simon our new dormitory mate, I'm Tenley", a childish giggle reverberated from her throat. He could tell from her accent that she originated from aristocracy, her well spoken voice accentuating words resonated only by those of the nobility.

"The girls have decided that I should come and welcome you to our family, well I don't literally mean family but your work colleagues, we like to think we are all one big family", and she let out an hysterical laugh.

"Why thank you for having me, I must say it is a pleasure to be here among such fine looking things" said Simon with a smile; again she erupted into a fit of giggles adding squeakily "your so cheeky".

At that she turned and walked back to her room, which was only a matter of feet away, he watched as she stepped into her room and whispered

"hope to see you later". Closing his own door he uttered -"a definite airhead, but a hell of a nice looking gal".

It turned out that Tenley shared the room with five other fine looking young ladies, their function at the hotel was as stable girls, they took any interested guests horse riding in the surrounding countryside, and of coarse looked after the animals.

'Janet and Janine', two Australian 'Sheila's working their way around Europe earning enough money for a world tour. Two South African springboks 'Bronwyn and Gemmia'- six foot tall Goddesses, slim with silvery black complexions. They were just passing through having lived in London for a year and were on the final leg of a two year stint in England. Then there was Eva a blonde Fraulein from Bavaria, Germany. She would have had no problem being mistaken for a lingerie model. Her father happened to be head chef in the hotel kitchen. All of the women were young aged between 19-20 years old and all were eager for new experiences. It did not take long for Simon to settle in his new surroundings but any thought he may have carried of being the centrepiece of this nice little Harem were quickly quelled . In one of the rooms that was mistakenly assumed to be a lavatory and without further inspection the presumption proved negative - resided Malcolm, the maître d' of the restaurant. A likable type who did in fact live just down the road in the village but preferred to stay rent free in the employees' accommodation at the hotel.

Malcolm was an ordinary character apart from going bald at the age of twenty three, he always answered a question with an -'eh', an idiom Simon found hilarious. He claimed he was a native New Zealander, this was evident in his hybrid accent, but had moved to the village when he was

ten years old, his paternal father originated in the village while his mother remained in the old country.

Life at the hotel was pretty mundane with everyone going about their assigned tasks. When he was not carrying guests' luggage to their allotted rooms Simon would be in the function hall preparing it for the next soirée. A fashion shoot where he would assist the photographer with his gear and lay out props. A wedding party, an engagement party, requiring planning for the positioning of large round tables with sittings of between eight and ten individuals.

On one occasion the top English automobile manufacturer 'Jaguar' held a motor show in the grounds of the hotel with all the latest models on show. This gave Simon the opportunity to drive these fantastically expensive cars, albeit around the grounds and into position onto the display rostrum; this added a little piece of glamour to the monotony.

The hotel work he discovered was seasonal and this tended to leave him with a lot of time twiddling his fingers and thumbs, to fill the void he would assist the head grounds man in his duties.

Douglas Fir a Yorkshire man in his fifties lived in the gatehouse with his wife, they had no children or none that anybody knew of.

Simon would mow the large manicured lawns, the freshly cut grass evoking images of a time when he was younger; prune the branches of the large oak and elm trees that lined the laneway to the hotel. The liquorice aromas of the chopped wood he cut for the magnificent fires in the lobbies permeated the air and filled his lungs with healthiness. The thorough cleaning of the many windows of the front and back of the hotel was but a few chores on an unending list.

Douglas it turned out was like a mentor who would keep Simon right in all his endeavours.

"hey lad don't hold the axe like that you do injury to yourself" he could be heard shouting at Simon as he attempted to chop the tree stumps into logs

"treat it wi respect and it will do job for you.

"You chopping with an axe is not just another job, there is an art to be mastered" cried Douglas and he took the offensive weapon from the young man and began to explain the so-called art.

Simon listened intently to the ramblings of this seemingly sane man going on about the dangers of lifting and swinging an axe when he heard Malcolm calling his name, "relief at last, saved by the bell" he mused to himself. "I'll have to go now I think I am required at the front desk", he accented to his teacher

-"right lad be here when you get back, only think about what I was saying, don't swing the axe, chop with the axe".

As he got to where Malcolm was he was greeted by his dorm buddy who was standing just before the entrance to the front lobby with an enormous grin between his cheeks.

"Who's a sly fox eh?

Who's a slippery dog eh?, who's a real dark horse eh"?

Simon was puzzled by his friend's assumptions,

"what are you talking about now",

enquired Simon Sanders scornfully.

"Eh? who is that at the front desk looking for you eh"? repeated Malcolm, almost implying the young man knew what he was talking about.

However he was perplexed, Simon was intrigued by the mystery and went to investigate his anonymous caller. On his approach to the reception room an eerie darkness lingered, hovering just above the door, stretching up the wall and back across the ornate ceiling; observing this for a nano second he quickly dismissed it from his consciousness and carried on through the opening. To his surprise there

sitting in a nondescript chair in reception was a face he recognised instantly, 'Donna Euryale'.

It had been two years since they last seen each other after his unceremonious exit from her home,. But "hell" thought he "she had fairly blossomed". Any romantic feelings he may have had for her had long since waned - however these notions soon awakened from their slumber at the sight and sound of her.

"But how did you know where I was, and why have you come here?" stuttering and stammering as he spoke.

She began to explain that she was baffled by his original disappearance without even a goodbye - how her father had said you were 'useless and far to old for her', of how your disappearing act should prove his point. But she had never lost faith and she knew deep down in her heart that Simon Sanders was the one for her.... She had also revealed that she had discovered his whereabouts from his former landlady who had given her his forwarding address, now she was here to bring him home.

Simon Sanders initial surprise quickly turned to anger at Donna Euryale's bold attitude.

"What do you mean you've come to take me home, what makes you think I want to go home? Just because you decide on the turn of a leaf that you want me back in your life I should just agree with you and like a little boy go running back to mammy".

It soon became clear to Donna Euryale that this was not the person she had known previously. She could also see that it was obvious in his tone that he was hurting, at the same time realising that she was not the source of his pain it was after all he that walked away from her.

The chill in the air eased and the two former lovers decided to walk around the grounds of the hotel for some one on one conversation away from the prying eyes and ears of his work colleagues.

The grounds as Simon Sanders had discovered during his many sojourns through them were extensive. As well as the grass tennis courts, the golf course and the cricket pitch with adjoining pavilion there were also gardens that displayed a wide variety of flowers and stone sculptures. Water features were also prominent, with small intricate streams channelled obscurely with great care quenching the widely dispersed shrubbery. Also hidden away in the undergrowth were secret passages leading to equally disguised doorways adorned with Doric columns that were cloaked with climbing ivy. Behind these were even more complicated and wondrous gardens that were he assumed the place were reflection and solicitude were easily obtained.

As Donna commented on the beauty of the countryside in which they strolled Simon Sanders admitted quietly to himself "he hadn't felt such anger in a long time", there was nothing in his new life to warrant feelings of such a twisted nature.

However when Donna Euryale began to speak of her hopes and fears the emotion in her voice, of which he still considered as angelic, stirred a reconcilable sympathy within him - the tears welled in her celestial eyes as she told him of her love for him and that it just grew stronger with his absence. She longed for his presence - revealing she could think of nothing else; her functioning as a person had come to a complete halt.

Simon Sanders could hardly believe what he was hearing but at the same time he could see she was an emotional wreck not the bubbly effervescent girl from yesteryear who had stole away his heart - he also could not ignore the fact she had lied to him. In so doing she had broken his trust a factor essential in any relationship between a man and a woman but because of her state he was willing to forego his

inner objections and let bygones be bygones. An old hackneyed phrase entered his reasoning,

'everyone deserves a second chance'. Despite his reservations Simon Sanders with a heavy heart decided to give their relationship a fresh start, but a hint of caution prevailed as he was quite aware of how quickly things in life can turn pear shaped.

CHAPTER TWENTY THREE

Life at the hotel resumed as normal although Donna was adamant she was not returning home without her beau, so for that purpose Simon managed to acquire a small rented house for her in the village some two miles from the hotel. He had explained to Donna that he had signed a contract of employment, pointing out to her he could not and would not just abandon his responsibilities. He was required to work a months notice and intended to fulfil his obligations.

"Anyway I promised the Aussie girls a game of tennis on the outdoor courts", he said to Donna Euryale with a wry grin.

"You do what you have to do", replied his increasingly frustrated ex partner", and promptly walked off to her rented accommodation.

"No wait don't be walking I will give you a lift", pleaded Simon Sanders. "Don't bother!" Came the reply in the distance. He stood perplexed watching as she disappeared into the trees, and almost with a sigh of relief he uttered "huh" turned and went back to his work duties.

With all of his troubles and idiosyncrasies resulting in a partial withdrawal from societal life, Simon still managed to maintain a modicum of charm with the ladies, his silvery tongue providing words the opposite sex longed to hear. He had talked his way into his neighbour's bedroom and had managed to gain their confidence; he would sit for hours and listen to their ramblings offering words of support if needed, all the while eyeing them greedily, but not quite taking advantage.

He also sensed the feelings were mutual. The Australian girls had offered to show him how to play tennis and when he accepted the game was arranged, and while he knew how

the game was played he was unprepared for the actual intricacies of this sport.

The previous months had seen him practice vociferously on how to hit a tennis ball which he found extremely difficult, despite these shortcomings he deemed himself ready and the game was on....The game itself was an event as it give all the staff some respite from attending and waiting on the sporadic and sometimes seldom seen guests. Simon trained hard and was to face Janet, one half of the Australian girls; Janine who was a budding artist/painter, having studied art in college, preferred to work on the abstract fresco of female-male figures frolicking at some unknown beach, this adorned the walls of the Jacuzzi, similar to Michaelangelo or Caravaggio she had been tasked by the hotel.

The Australians trained very little declaring themselves experts at the sport having played it from a young age. After a gruelling training session Simon made his way to kitchen where he would sit on one of the many service tables and observe the chefs at their work. One evening he was joined by Miss Farington who sat and conferred with him on his progress;

"is there anything you require?", she asked.

"No, I just hope my nerves don't get the better of me tomorrow and my performance is spot on".

"Oh I'm sure you will be fine don't be worrying so much," said she reassuringly.

"Talking of performance Simon Sanders, tell me, how big is yours?", said she alluringly.

Simon sat on motionless trying to figure out what was had just been implied of him;

"is she trying to seduce me the night before a big game?" he accented. Unsure of a proper response he stammered and spluttered the saliva dropping uninvitingly onto his shorts and bare thigh,

"ah, would you like to find out?", he whispered, turning to look in her ravenous eyes

"well you look so fit in those shorts and I can think of no better way to relax you. Why don't you pop down to the cellar and pick a nice bottle of red wine and make you way to my room". Simon did not need to be asked twice, in a whisper he was off to the cellar and knocking on her door before she had time to remove her slinky black dress. They sat in her room for hours talking, drinking wine and generally getting to know each other. Simon went to the cellar on two more occasions, after the talk there was a rashion of passion, which lasted into the small hours. Early next morning miss Farington dressed went down to her office and advised Simon to do the same, get ready for his big game.

He sat in his room and a think tank developed in his mind over the previous night events, "it is as if she is aware of my intentions and this was her way of saying goodbye", thought he. When he thought some more he cringed at these suggestions, "what I'm I thinking about?, how the hell was she supposed to be aware of my plans? Nothing was indicated nor implied, maybe subconsciously she could tell be my demeanour"; this inquisition continued as he got himself ready for his big debut.

Gradually and slowly these thoughts ebbed and flowed before finally lessening and fading from view. The game its self was watched by most of the staff who cheered on their own particular character, however it soon turned out to be an anti-climax as the young sportsman's performance was sluggish and lethargic, as if he had no energy. Afterwards Simon retired to his room where he fell into a coma for twelve hours.

The next day he set about the unenviable task of informing his employers of his decision to leave the hotel and return home. There were no goodbyes or farewells and

after having worked his required notice he and Donna Euryale were on a flight to their native land.

While onboard they both talked about their future together, Donna ever the chatterbox painted an impressive picture, enthusing that they should wait no more than a year before they should marry. Not wanting to seem unreasonable Simon agreed to every her whim, the perfect relationship thought his spouse to be.

He then became painfully aware of a terrible conundrum,

"hold on a minute", he grumbled "this is all very enlightening but where am I to stay? Where am I going to live until these plans come to fruition", he was perplexed at his lack of planning and oversight.

"Don't worry" whispered Donna Euryale in a tone of complete assurance. "We are going to live at my grandmothers house, she has been diagnosed with a mild form of dementia and has had to go into a care home, she wont be coming out of it and my parents have decided I should live there, it will be our home. This revelation drew a deep concern from Simon as he pondered, "such a callous family, so cold and selfish"; this blatant lack of empathy only strengthened his opinion that this brood were only out to get what they wanted in life even if it meant discarding family members. However distasteful this scenario may have appeared he determined,

"mine is not to question, only to reason why".

Chapter Twenty four

The groundwork prepared it was just a matter of moving in together and letting fate run it's course, all doubts had to be cast aside in this fait accompli; a .process of the mental maturing of Simon Sanders had commenced, he would have to leave his childish methods of deduction where they belonged, in puberty. and concentrate on the present, in

effect he had to grow up and make a go of the hand he was dealt.

After six months of living with Donna Euryale when there when many arguments over one thing or another which he instead of turning his back and walking away, faced down and sought to iron out the different opinions between opposing sides, in so doing he felt his adulthood impose itself.

A re-enforcement of this attitude was strengthened by the news that his partner had become pregnant; Donna Euryale was eight weeks with child indicating an infant's presence would be in their midst. Simon Sanders was delighted at the thought of becoming a father, reasoning, perhaps this could inject some order into their somewhat chaotic lives. It could also prove the perfect incentive for them to get married as Simon readily acknowledged in a whisper, "I'm not getting any younger". He had just turned thirty years of age and unusually for someone to reach such a milestone in life he had not one thing to show for his achievements thus far; this realisation sparked an analytical assassination of his fragile character.

Who in life was to blame for his shortcomings? There were many suspects who were culpable-his school teacher Fishy Doc whose strange behaviour and weird mannerisms were a thunder bolt from the heavens; even though it had been over twenty years since encountering this eccentric man his impact had a lasting profundity. This was the first real authority figure who through his actions taught Simon Sanders to disrespect not respect his elders.

A miasma of deeply disturbing thoughts now clawed their way through the intricate channels of his conscious mind like small African army ants incessantly pursuing their prey. The disgusting behaviour of HS who assaulted and insulted his very being-the folly of his wayward friends Sammy Sercle, Dickey Nolan and the soul less figure of

Tucker the fucker; while these characters had a rebellious streak they were all imbued with a tinge of innocence. The affliction of images tormented him and he freely admitted that maybe he was as bad his unfortunate compatriots who had paid the ultimate price, their demise hauntingly stalked him and he could not escape their chilling grasp.

Interspersed with these jungle demons were the pleasantries of Stephen Unlike whose innocent banter seemed a million miles away from where Simon continually found himself; he was racked with 'if only' as he pondered Lamia who appeared even more exquisite and delectable in the middle of all of his turmoil. In the survey of his mind he replayed over and over her mindless depravity and his enjoyment of her wanton desires, there was no way he could attribute Lamia's contribution to his bouts of temporary insanity.

A different set of thoughts surfaced of which he could conceivably apportion blame-the indiscriminate appearance and disappearance of his father, his ultimate witnessing of his fathers untimely and grotesquely horrible death. This cruel event he determined was directly responsible for his mother's descent into the abyss of madness and concluding death.

He could have attributed any of these factors for his downward spiral of unruliness and each on their own were major contributors, however, it appeared to his realisation that the catalysis for his disruptiveness was undoubtedly the perverse actions of HS. This man had inflicted a trauma so alien and incomprehensible that without his inner strength he would have without question lost his battle for survival in his youth, for every action there is an equal and opposite reaction was his ultimate determining.

These feelings had a danger of ruining the relationship with Donna Euryale, he ceased to beat himself up and ended his character assassination and thought about the bigger

picture, he was soon to become a father and needed to display passion to her , she required a man not a dribbling boy. Time came and went and she gave birth to a healthy baby girl and both parents were elated at her arrival and even though Donna Euryale had never met his mother she decided to name her Bridgeen in respect of Simon's wishes; their journey to parenthood had begun. It seemed as if he was not wasting time as she soon fell pregnant again and within a year had given birth to another healthy girl; in keeping with tradition they both agreed to name her Lucy.

The track was laid and they continued on their wondrous journey and were often seen about the town with their two daughters, because of this companionship and togetherness they decided to announce a date for their wedding; soon they would be united under one name, Sanders. Donna Euryale was a little apprehensive about dropping her fathers name and although she was aware of a practice of young married women keeping a double-barrelled surname as in Donna Euryale Sanders, once she got used to the name she decided Donna Sanders had a certain honest and homely ring to it.

Through all of this bliss Donna Euryale although she would never admit it partly due to the fact she was unaware of it was afflicted with postnatal depression, which usually occurs after childbirth, because she had given birth in quick succession she was suffering now with a double dose with delayed onset. It hit her with a vengeance and she became extremely irritable and withdrawn - in this situation Simon Sanders was supposed to be a mind reader and be aware of her condition; even though he did not know he should have known and reacted accordingly. And while his lack of knowledge irritated the situation his best recourse was to take the girls out for a walk adding -"come ladies your mum needs to go for a nap" speaking as he did as if the girls understood him.

He would usually take them to the park allow them to play on the swings, slides and every thing else that was there to keep them occupied and when they had tired themselves out he would strap them in the double pram and saunter on home. Occasionally he would stop off at his favourite coffee shop in the town for an indulgent milky cappuccino and some quiet reflection, the same one where his mother used to go.

As he busily negotiated the door of the café trying his best not to disturb the two sleeping beauties he came face to face with a sight that took his breath away.

HS sat at the small table he used to meet his mother for their weekly rendezvous. Not bothering to raise his eyes from the newspaper or magazine he was reading this devil of a man sipped casually from his tea cup seemingly carefree and without a worry in the world. Simon's first reaction was to flee, to run away as so often had been the case before when faced with difficult situations, however, he quickly came to a recognition this action solves nothing, he had learned from experience and if he did not confront the demon monkey on his back it would haunt him for all eternity.

Quickly and silently he pushed the pram further into the coffee shop finding a bench chair he promptly sat down. His inner thoughts congratulated his bravery as if he had just competed some amazing feat; then just as he contemplated his next move the pangs of self-doubt entered his realm. A cold chill hurried through his quivering frame, and like the run off of a heavy shower escaping down a culvert he felt the blood drain from his once confident smiling features. His breathing became intermittent and constricted as he felt the tightening of his chest, it was apparent, his panic attack was in full swing. Fortunately for him the coffee shop was quiet with only a handful of people sitting about quietly chatting, no-one it appeared had observed his

transformation, luckier still his two angels had not stirred and were happily still sleeping.

Flashbacks and disturbing memories infiltrated his consciousness and an uncomfortable warmth descended on his person. Simon had been unaware of this happening for some time now, he had been pre-occupied with other matters and had not had the time to think of such nightmarish events but now with the re-appearance of HS it was time to confront and dispatch to hell his tormenter.

After a period his composure returned and he approached his perceived torturer, trembling with sweaty palms he stood in front of him. With an unbelievable air of confidence bordering on complete arrogance HS lifted his gaze toward him,

"ah my boy how have you been, I didn't see or hear you come in"; the chilling menace blatantly obvious as the words slithered and dripped from his loathsome mouth.

"What the hell are you doing here?", demanded an irate Simon. "Why on earth have you returned? Your presence in this town is not welcome", the younger mans face reddened, he felt his blood boil.

"You", continued Simon Sanders, "almost, and if I had not have been stronger, you would have destroyed my life with your despicable antics, because of you I feel mentally insane."

"What are you talking about boy? I have never done anything to you that you did not secretly want." The young man could not comprehend what he was hearing from this vile individual. Was he implying that Simon as a young boy asked to have his childhood, all his hopes and dreams snatched away because of this child molester's deviant desires.

"What was wrong eh, could you not find yourself a woman that you had to satisfy your abnormal urges on an innocent child? It is not help you need, no' you need to have

your throat sliced open with a large knife you fucking imbecile."

His outburst had caught the interest of the few people who were in the café and he suddenly became aware of all the eyes fixated upon him. And although they may have been just concerned onlookers the paranoia that had dogged him his whole waking life overwhelmed and subdued his tirade.

"Calm down" offered HS, "I can see you are uptight about something but I only returned because I am ill. I had been away working in America and I don't want to die alone in a foreign country; your brother Billy has suggested that I stay with him just until I get myself sorted and that is my intention."

"Déjà vu", murmured Simon, his eyeballs bulging almost detaching themselves from their sockets, the veins in his neck and arms throbbing as if ready to burst. He was appalled at what he was hearing, "what do you mean until you get yourself sorted?" as he recalled, "those are the exact words you used to my mother some twenty five years ago when you came to stay at our home". "Well if I have anything to do with it you'll be staying well clear of my family" adding as an afterthought, "what is left of it."

He kicked the table HS was sitting at so hard that the tea cup that was sitting quietly and was full of hot tea lifted off it's saucer spilled it's contents over this despicable man and crashed to the floor, the clattering of a metal tea pot on the tiled floor completed the scene.

"Stay away from me and stay away from my family"; he uttered with a certain malice, before collecting his children and angrily leaving the premises.

Making his way home Simon Sanders emotions were in a state of high alert, walking furiously he felt the pent-up anger rage in his head. Twenty years of frustration had been unleashed on an unsuspecting public, albeit a few patrons of

a coffee house. But he did not care his normal conservative attitude of not wanting to disturb the peace by just accepting the absurdity of Joe public's ridiculous responses and opinions was beginning to wane. All his life he had been reluctant to offend what he considered the incongruity of stupidity-effectively he had been held back by a paranoia imposed maliciously and selfishly by an alien being-HS had a lot to answer for.

CHAPTER TWENTY FOUR

Simon parked the pram beside a bench positioned in a rest and relaxation area on the way to his home and sat down to consider what had just occurred. As he sat with his head in his hands he began to tremble as the visions of HS invaded his waking thoughts, a nauseating stench arrived provoking a feeling of wanting to be physically ill. Did he just confront his tormenter permeated his thinking and however liberated he should have felt an intense fear welled within.

This man had been the cause of all of his failings in life-had caused him to miss out on so much, had fled in fear of discovery leaving a trail of destruction so devastating it was a wonder Simon Sanders had survived thus far. Now he had returned to the fold and by implication was weaning his way back into the family to possibly inflict further damage on a third generation. Gathering his thoughts Simon Sanders regained his equilibrium and made his way home to spread the news of what had just occurred. As he entered his home he was greeted by his wife who, shocked at the state he was in hysterically enquired on the health of her two beloved children.

"No everything is ok, I just took a turn for the worst, must have been the chocolate cake I had with my coffee at the café". Simon and Donna went into meaningless conversation of how standards where dropping at the coffee shop and of how they should be reported to the health and safety authority.

He determined that he did not want to alarm her by informing her of what truly happened - this was an internal family crisis - equally this decision was hard to justify.

A mini crisis averted they continued to talk about nothing in particular a trait Simon really admired in his wife that she could hold a conversation with him on any subject trivial or otherwise, the comfort was mutual. After preparing their two daughters for bed Donna Euryale retired for the evening leaving Simon to enjoy his favourite past-time alone watching TV.

He sat looking at the screen thinking about the day's events, he could not believe his brother had agreed to put such an evil man up in his own home but he also realised that his brother was ignorant to the ways of this so called uncle. There was a further troubling aspect to this, Billy who had returned home a few years earlier with a wife and family had two young sons of his own. Billy junior who was ten years of age and the younger of the two Oliver who was eight; Simon felt obliged to inform him of the monster in his midst, but as it was such a late hour he decided to speak to his brother early next morning.

He had very little sleep that night as images of HS tormented his closed sockets - picking up the phone he dialled his brother's number. "Hello" answered the receiver as the connection was made,

"hello Billy", Simon replied, how's things?,

"ah what's the crack stranger, I have not heard from you in a while" said his elder. They conversed on a wide range of subjects, the banality supreme.

"I believe you have a guest staying with you" enquired Simon, the annoyance in his tone oblivious to his brother;

"oh you mean uncle Hugh", he uttered in a sort of surprised way, -"no he has gone, he was only here for a week he has managed to get a flat in the town; as a matter of fact he has moved into the flat above the shop where you used to live. Apparently Ivan Koniving and he are old friends and he has let him stay there rent free, how's that for a bit of good fortune".

"What?" Simon was livid on hearing this news, not because of the fortunate circumstances, he was the first to acknowledge that sometimes these things happen in life; he was painfully angry because he had struggled with life's idiosyncrasies since his inclusion on the roll call of existence. Mr good luck had continually passed him by- 'The wheel of fortune', it seemed refused to stop at his door and he was furious.

He thought of how all his life he's had to beg, steal or borrow, scrimp and save to get by on the crumbs from the big table and here to add insult to injury his tormenter, who was bereft of remorse was having it handed to him on a plate.

"Well isn't that just typical", said an increasingly angry Simon Sanders "someone who never works a day in their lives ends up being lifted and pampered

"What's got up your nose?", enquired Billy, "sounds like Mr envy has arrived".

"Who me?, no I just think it is a crying shame that some of us have had to work all our days and still have nothing to show for it; along comes this bum beat, fresh off the banana boat and lands a plum residence without even working up a sweat; it is just so unfair".

Simon Sanders cogitated over this as Billy continued to waffle on the phone - he listened as his brother advised and suggested that he shouldn't be so hard on his unfortunate uncle.

"If you think he was lucky by landing that flat rent free you are going to love hearing this", said Billy Sanders with a hint of glee in his voice; Simon could see a large grin appearing on his receiver, sent it seems down the line from his brother, -

"because he claims he is ill he has been given a large sickness benefit from a previous employer in order to re-

habilitate his condition, a condition it appears no one can diagnose the actual problem".

A nauseating sensation overwhelmed Simon on hearing this,

"that bastard is at it again" he murmured, taking the mouthpiece away from his mouth

"what was that you said?, I never heard, your voice seemed to be muffled", asked his brother.

"Oh nothing" replied Simon, "look I will have to go there is someone at the front door I will speak to you soon", and he ended the call. Billy was left puzzled at his abruptness, he had an inkling his younger brother was going to confide something to him, however, this notion quickly left him and he went on about his daily business.

"That con man was playing the 'God' help me card, the sympathy card" growled Simon silently and angrily - he was going around telling everyone he was ill, not only was he on a sympathy trip but he had also managed to fool even members of Simon's own family with his apparent lies and deceit.

In retrospect it could have been perceived that Simon was in fact envious of the fact that his so-called uncle was being treated with compassion because of his mystery illness, invariably this tends to lead people into becoming more empathetic and more generous to the point that they have a propensity to give anything that is asked of them. As far as his former residence above the shop was concerned it was highly unlikely that he would ever have returned to that-he was of the opinion of going forward not backward; he would hardly go back to a place he deemed uninhabitable. The absurdity of the notion that he was jealous of his stroke of good fortune was a further unfounded idea.

Because of HS's previous actions, Simon had to struggle through his school years without direction or focus,

concentrating his thoughts on trying to comprehend the evil being done to him instead of living for life and work. Honing a particular aptitude developed from his tastes; a bricklayer, a plumber or an electrician, or any of the number of trades that were available for him to avail of-an opportunity wasted. He found asking for assistance particularity distasteful and for this the reason why he worked at so many menial occupations for a pittance of wages.

During this period of inner conflict the relationship with his wife slowly and surely became increasingly strained; he would shout and raise his voice in her presence frightening not only Donna Euryale but also alarming the children as well. So much so that she, who was the epitome of understanding would often take the children to her parents for days on end to escape his rants. To add fuel to this tenseness alcohol soon became equidistant to the problem - Simon who had vowed never to repeat the mistakes of his mother by finding the answer at the bottom of the bottle turned to the demon drink to find solace, often alienating those most closest to him in the process.

While he was on one of his binges if he was not at home causing uproar he would go to his secret place, secret to him obvious to all who knew him. A place in the wood behind his home where after constructing a small makeshift hide complete with tree stump for a chair he would go and drink himself legless; Donna Euryale cared little at least he was out of her hair. Simon stood accused of narrow minded selfishness by his contemporaries, because of his behaviour, equally his level of abuse directly or indirectly aimed at friends and relatives he blamed on a lack of understanding of his acute problems; but if they did not know they did not know due to his desire for privacy.

On one of his soirée's he found himself outside the front door of his former abode where his tormenter now resided;

consciously or unconsciously he made the decision to confront his abuser. Retribution in mind he climbed the stairs and knocked profusely on the door, no time for sentiment he had come this far. Opening the door slightly and peering through the small slit HS breathed a sigh of relief,

"oh it is you my boy" and opened the door further,

"who were you expecting" gasped Simon sanders sarcastically, "the police, or a broken down shattered shadow of a man who once had his whole life in front of him until you got your greasy disgusting hands on him?". Although he was incoherent he still managed to utter these words in one uninterrupted breath, adding slowly controllably, with aplomb "you stole my life!!".

He could no longer listen to his denials or his nonchalant dismissal of accusations

"do you know what you have done to me? I'm a broken down engine in need of constant repair because of you, you fucking imbecile"; as well as a verbal attack on HS in which he invariably attempted to deny all knowledge, Simon Sanders began a tough physical assault and lashed out at him. Again and again he rained punches onto him and was surprisingly accurate with his throws. He became even more enraged when he attempted to fight back, however, this was more of an act of bravado than actual defence, typical of a coward; along with the punches he started to kick him all about his lower body until he was on the ground cowering in submission.

Twenty years of pent up aggression unleashed onto this excuse for a man in an uncontrollable fashion and when it was over a silence hung in the room as Simon Sanders surveyed the scene.

Standing with clenched fists a dishevelled appearance and a foam like substance around his mouth he glared over HS who by now was curled foetus like on the floor - he

realised this insignificant worthless piece of shit was not the big scary ogre who had held him to ransom in his childhood. He wasn't the ten foot tall evil monster from his conscious and unconscious nightmares that had scared the bjesus out of him, forcing a young directionless boy on a never ending road to no-where. A few expletives later Simon was off out the door, down the stairs disappearing into the cool night where he walked around aimlessly figuring his next move.

Making his way home he reflected on what had just occurred, although relieved he had confronted the evil demonic one he still felt anger at the display of defiance from his tormenter; he began to fume and a red mist descended as the bull charges it's matador. His blood still on a rolling simmer as he thought of HS and his lack of remorse. "Well that does not matter" he thought , "that's it, end of, I have got my vengeance albeit 20 years overdue, if that blood sucker has any sense he will be out of that rat trap immediately or he should face the same wrath".

Walking into an empty house, which had not bothered him before he began to comprehend the damage he had caused to his wife. looking around the living room, which was once full of life and laughter he realised his selfish behaviour and uncontrollable rage had driven his family away. no ifs, no buts, or ands, he and he alone was responsible. Simon Sanders knew he had some major grovelling to do if there was to be any chance of reconciliation with his Donna Euryale Sanders and he resolved to put things right.

He sat down in a chair and started to sketch a plan in his mind on how to bring his wife home and as he thought an emotional whirlwind stirred within as flashbacks and images of better times with her flooded his memories. Days on the beach, playful times in the water as it ebbed and flowed with the time, sitting down in the hotel lobby and

playing bingo with her and the rest of the guests. Some memories are meant to be locked away; this particular memory made him cringe at the thought of it, however, it also invoked feelings of happiness as he recalled he checked at the bingo winning them a sumptuous free meal in the hotel restaurant, adding as it did to the perfection of their first holiday together.

Without warning he began to sob, just a trickle at first with a single tear falling gently from his watery eyes; slowly methodically the tears began the flow of a torrent and he started to wail profusely. He could not understand why this was, he hadn't cried this much before even when his parents had passed away. Holding his head in his hands he began to question himself

"what the hell is wrong with me, What have I don't to deserve this?" he asked through the tears, the self-pity reeked from his pores,

"why me?", he implored of some unseen presence. A melancholy shrouded him and he sat back in the chair and closed his eyes - falling into a restless sleep.

Next morning opening his eyes he felt a strange euphoria as the rays of sunlight shone brightly through the half pulled curtains. Whereas usually after a hard night of drinking and sleeping uncomfortably downstairs in a chair he would awake with a powerful hangover, a painful creak in his neck and would complain to anybody who would listen of how he had seriously injured himself.

"Self-inflicted" were the utterances of his unsympathetic wife. A cool calm serenity enveloped his person as he pictured a brave new beginning - he had no idea why he was so elated and even though he was not hung over from an expected hang over he felt an extremely heavy weight had been raised from his shoulders the beginnings of a brave new day echoed in his mind. With that thought he set about making himself some breakfast.

Standing before the opened fridge door he cast his beady eyes over it's contents which were slim to say the least. Eggs, a half eaten ham and a few past their sell by date tomatoes sat on the sparsely populated shelf. As so often the case he couldn't decide on which to choose, a particular nuance in himself he found frustrating and mind numbing. Occasionally breakfast time would be over and he found it nearing lunchtime through his indecision.

Listening to the radio a soothing satisfaction took hold as he attempted to add purpose to this dilemma; declaring the moment too crucial to listen to the essential classics station he turned the dial and tuned into a more upbeat, some might say a more common radio station, one that plays music for the less discernable palate. Tottering in and around the opened fridge door a tune he recognised began to play and leaning over to adjust the volume he listened to the quaint little tune 'Tell Me There's A Heaven'. A melancholic song concerning the death of a child, its premise being that you should not worry as there is indeed a Heaven; "a song close to my heart", he quietly said as he carried on his tortuousness.

As this internal debate raged he was interrupted by the ringing of the front doorbell; "saved at last" he murmured, closed the fridge and went to answer the door.

Standing on his front porch there was a uniformed police officer and another man in a dark grey inexpensive looking suit, white shirt and matching tie. Both men carried seriously grim expressions and they spoke in equally monotonous tones.

"Hello" lumbered the officer',

'hmm', grunted Simon half expecting bad news--

"we are here enquiring after a Mr Simon Sanders - is he here?"

continued the officer…

"in connection with what" replied a slow burning and angry Simon

A look of dismay appeared on the officers face, it was clear he was affronted at the tone the present conversation was taking - the second man then interrupted, speaking calmly he offered;

"Sir we have a matter of great delicacy to confer on you may we come in?".

"oh okay if you must"

his annoyance apparent as he led them into the living room.

The grey suited man began by introducing both of them,

"sir this is Sergeant Law of the child protection unit and I am Mr Justin Lacaless from the public prosecution service, we are here over an incident which occurred last night"

"really" murmured Simon "what incident would that be and how can I be of help? he uttered defiantly. Silently he knew what Mr Lacaless was referring to, however, as far as he was concerned it was a private personal matter the authorities had no right to be involved in.

"Sir", continued Lacaless, we have had a Mr Hugh Sanders under surveillance ever since his return to this country from America, where he served a jail sentence for the sexual assault of a young wheelchair bound handicapped boy. Our counterparts in America have labelled him a serial sex offender which leads us to believe his nefarious activities may have had an impact on you!".

The droning of Justin Lacaless monologue started to irritate Simon and he felt the beginnings of a cold sweat emanate from his pores; his anxiety levels increased and he could sense the four walls contract and pulsate as they closed in to surround him.

"No!", he blurted out, imagining as he did a barrage of questions floating above him, swaying and contorting in mid-air before descending upon him, seeking answers.

"No!" cried he again, "I will not have my public life put on display for all to see, this is a private matter, I am a nobody and accordingly wish to remain". This defiant display of reluctance was in Sergeant Laws view perfectly understandable as he quietly noted, "no one wants their dirty laundry aired in public, that is, unless they have voyeuristic tendencies".

"Now now young man no-one wants to put you in the shop window, all we want is some assistance in putting this miscreant behinds bars," offered Sergeant Laws after his secret thought, his deep monotone voice pleasingly reassuring....

Again Simon flatly refused to comply eventually asking the men to leave telling them he could be of no assistance to them. Walking out of the house the men's frustration was apparent in the manner in which they left, similar to that of an unfinished masterpiece; Mr Lacaless enquired of Simon had he heard from his brother Billy? when he replied no, Mr Lacaless let it drop casually that his brother had been in to the police station to make a complaint of some nature.

"What, when?" insisted an overly eager Simon;

"sorry sir we can't divulge the substance of our complaints", enthused Justin Lacaless, and with a blasé air in his step walked away.

This information intrigued and puzzled Simon, "what was his brother complaining to the law about" thought he; "it was not like him to ask the police for anything, he considered the local force biased and one sided in their approach to grievances from society at large.

"They are just trying to nose into your business in an attempt to find out any minor infractions or dirty dealings" was Billy's old war cry; the police in his view acted on ill-judged information provided by even more unscrupulous characters. He had himself been a victim of a so-called telephone informant, where members of the public phoned

the police anonymously accusing Billy of owning an unlicensed motor vehicle. While there was a semblance of truth surrounding this it was later established that he had in fact just purchased the vehicle and had not got round to the necessaries due to it being a weekend. This did not stop the police intrusion going through his life with a fine toothcomb looking for ill-gotten gains, only for none to be found.

For Simon it seemed unthinkable that his brother would have went to them at all, so when he telephoned his brother to enquire of the situation he was soon put in the picture.

Billy seemed distant almost coy as he spoke to his brother on the phone, he avoided any mention of the police and presumed not to know what Simon was asking of him;

"come on Billy the police where at my door enquiring of HS, what dealings have you had with him", the frustration in his phone manner apparent in his tone. After a long silence Billy finally divulged their meeting.

"That bastard has been tampering with my son while he was staying here, the dirty evil scoundrel; not only that, Oliver had his friend Sean staying for a sleep over and he attempted to molest him the fucking monkey.

"Okay brother calm down you will give yourself a hernia if you don't relax", said Simon reassuringly.

The conversation continued on these lines and Simon by now was feeling the beginnings of a cold sweat as it slowly flowed over his trembling body; an asphyxiating contorted sensation overwhelming him as his anxiety levels gradually started to increase. He was fully aware that he could have prevented the machinations of this sexual deviant by speaking up-but what was he to say? Who could he have told and not feel a certain shame, an embarrassment of humiliation to shame all shame. He had lived with this secret for over twenty years and although his peculiarities didn't go unnoticed who would have believed HS was his

tormentor; with this dilemma raging in his mind he still managed to console his brother.

Not wanting to appear insensitive Simon calmly asked of Billy how he came to such an assertion; his brother replied

"well the monkey crept into their room in the dead of night and started to fumble under their bedclothes. When the boys, who were scared witless by this ominous figure in the dark, challenged him he claimed to be looking for a cigarette lighter; a cigarette lighter!, under their bedclothes - the fucking monkey". He could hear clearly an emotional Billy as he almost but not quite fully started to weep.

Meanwhile as abruptly and brazenly as HS had arrived at his nephew's home seeking solace so too did he leave; HS had fled with his meagre belongings his whereabouts unknown to those concerned on such matters.

Later it transpired he had gone to a half way house which deals with tramps and vagabonds and who among its many cash donating patrons was Ivan Koniving. He had contributed on a regular basis to a project aimed at assisting the homeless and who in turn seek to find such less fortunate members of society accommodation. An ironic sentiment unfolded, Billy was aware of the work carried out by Ivan Koniving and was also vaguely aware that he knew his uncle HS, Simon it appeared was completely oblivious to the connection.

The police became regular visitors to Simon's home, surmising, probing, enquiring as to the reasons to his cavalier dismissal of their efforts to bring prosecution upon HS. A number of weeks passed in which they finally apprehended their man, he was deemed a high risk offender and promptly remanded into custody; however, and a number of the care unit team were extremely concerned about his lack of restrictions although expressed it privately. The supposedly secure prison into which he was placed was in fact another half way house with admittedly more

constraints on its inhabitants; it had maybe one or two more bars on the windows and a large front door which was locked after ten o clock at night. Prisoners, inmates, residents call them what you will, were not confined to locked cells but were able to mingle freely and associate on a one to one basis, sharing all the modern conveniences even the worst offender could avail of.

CHAPTER TWENTY FIVE

This was definitely a tense period of reflection and contemplation for anyone connected to the case; the ramifications were huge for the family as a whole. For his part Simon did not fully appreciate the stigma attached to the revelations that had been unwrapped, those that were slowly uncovering the debauchery of one of their own; the close family, of which there were many, declared their unending support, he was aware however how others would interpret such nastiness. One person he could rely on not to be judgemental was his younger sister Roberta who he now confided in on a regular basis; and although she never fully understood the concept, having been shielded and protected all her life she became his rock.

Standing alone in the kitchen of his now empty house he thought about his day in court and of his nervousness at confronting his attacker again. His mind was awash with muddle as he went to answer the telephone, which had been ringing unnoticed for what seemed an eternity;

"hullo" said he picking up the receiver,

"hello, Simon its Billy, how's things"?.

"Oh, yeah fine, can't complain" answered his younger brother. "Well you better get yourself over to grandma's house y our sister has just dropped dead"....

That was it that was how he learned of the demise of his beautiful if somewhat flawed sibling; she had reached her twentieth year and now her short life had expired, without, it appeared an apologetic hint from our 'God'.

However much it was expected, the family were told from an early stage in Roberta's life that her time on this earth was minimal, it was still a bolt from the blue. A surreal atmosphere took hold as all involved tried to

understand the inexplicable destruction current in the family Sanders, none more so than Simon Sanders; it had been a difficult and heart wrenching experience to lose both his makers so early in life's crusade. The trauma of losing his youngest and only sister who it has to be said had barely lived, almost but not quite neared him to the brink. This episode also managed to bring all of the brothers together as they united in their grief; in so doing they probed, articulated and searched for answers.

Through this process it emerged there was not a lot anyone could have done to prevent their sisters death bar giving her a complete heart transplant as one of her doctors explained; the only way she could maybe have survived was if she had have been in hospital at the time of her seizure. At the same time explained the doctor -"the quality of her existence would have been low, comparable only to a vegetative state, where most probable she would have been brain dead". None of the brothers would have wished this scenario and agreed it was for all intents and purposes for the best.

However, the eldest of the three brothers was angry and confused, David accented that if her heart had been maintained as it should have been with regular check-ups and proper medicine she could have survived. The remaining brothers were in total agreement but they also pointed out that they weren't in the know as this information remained in the realm of their dead parents.

Funeral arrangements were made and Roberta was interred with her late mother and father; and as before life attempted return to normal. While not the most appropriate of delays it did provide a welcome respite in the events occurring elsewhere in Simon's turmoil

During this period and after tense rounds of questioning the police charged HS with the attempted molestation of minors, alleging that he Hugh Sanders in his own

Machiavellian miscreant manner allegedly tried to interfere-cause sexual abuse on the persons of Oliver Sanders and his young friend Sean Ergoline. However, and the police were emphatic in their indications to Simon, the evidence was flimsy as HS denied all knowledge of the boys allegations; no member of the judiciary was going to convict albeit a repeat offender on the word of minors.

This was extremely troubling for Simon as after unloading a burden he had carried alone most of his life, a burden it has to be added was far to excessive for one person. He was being asked to take one more giant leap in the interests of justice, revealing along the way the skeletons in his closet. In so doing unearthing his inner most secrets.

After much soul searching where he spent many nights enduring the anxiety attacks and cold sweats, imagining the blood as it seeped and trickled from pores on his forehead his reluctance was absolute; although this position gradually softened as he realised any negative decision from him would have a devastating impact on the boys. He expressed quietly to himself

"why should I go forth and expose this deviant of a man?, no-one assisted me in my hour of need"; this thought provoking scenario had the potential of enwrapping and entangling the flashing neurons skipping across his brain leading to confusing thoughts; as he assented,

"who am I to bring this kind of shame upon my father's good name?". This was the dilemma he now faced but there was one positive; the self-loathing and quirky indifference he had experienced all his life and which had held him back from most if not all of his endeavours was slowly ebbing from his psyche.

The hopeless feelings of guilt however ingrained in the axons of his mind wilted and withered, he quickly and assuredly realised he had nothing to be ashamed of, he after

all had done nothing wrong except expose a beast from within. Although he was unaware of it at the time his actions carried heroic undertones, he recalled the conversation he had with himself on his flight to England when he battled his doubters and detractors. His mind in a state of uncertainly, constantly urging and willing him to go home; only now did he realise the importance of his presence in his home environment. Simon Sanders true calling was and had been, however painful, to expose the machinations of his devilish uncle. His epiphany realised he became aware his parents were watching, the angels on his shoulders.

The Chief Public Prosecutor had requested a meeting with him to discuss strategy, a plan of action for the court room, more importantly to temper his behaviour in front of a crown court judge.

Sitting in the office of the Cpp, the man explained the etiquette of the judge's domain "at all times the Lord has to addressed as your honour, there is to be no farting, swearing or burping. Answer a direct question with a simple yes or no and on no account argue with the prosecutor or the defence lawyer".

The Cpp was a tall man standing 6'4", aged approximately fifty or fifty five years old bald on top with a skirting of what used to be presumably a thick matt of greyish black hair along his sides. His round face was offset with a pair of black and grey rimmed square framed eyeglasses and a growth of hair covered what was undoubtedly a double chin; although not overly overweight there was a certain starchy roundness in his posture. His dark coloured eyes conveyed an austerely gaze and his deep base sounding voice carried a calm authoritative tone; he was known only to those in the know and was labelled 'The Chief Public Prosecutor'.

"You will hear some unsavoury revelations and false accusations in an attempt to discredit you", explained he to Simon. "On no account do you use the word liar in the court room, it is a court of law not an inquisition. Regardless of his guilt he is innocent until proven guilty and that is your que to damn him to hell". Simon was taken aback at this use of language but queried no more assuming "this must be how it is done".

The day of the hearing arrived and a nervous Simon sat patiently outside court number two shuffling and fumbling unable to string two coherent sensible thoughts together in the mesh of dendrites. Scanning the waiting area he watched the comings and goings of a plethora of bodies as they rushed back and forth and up and down the silvery grey corridor entering and exiting various doors indicating rooms of purpose. Out of this mix he heard his name being called by an unknown voice, unsure and confused he stood up from his chair to greet the mystery pursuer   "Hello Simon - Simon Sanders?" "yes, yes that's me" replied a nervous boy; "hi how are you, my name is Aurora plains, I am a lawyer of the CPP and I was suppose to represent you in court today";

"supposed to represent me? why has something happened that you are not?" said he.

"Well yes", she continued, "there will be no need for you to attend the proceedings your alleged abuser has indicated he is willing to admit all charges against you for a lesser sentence".

A furious Simon raged

"what!, is that it, what about the reason I decided to give evidence, my young nephew and his friend?"

"that will be dealt with also but separate from you, at least we got him for you", adding as an afterthought, "you should be grateful". -"that's just typical" asserted Simon Sanders.

****

Because of the seriousness of the offences, the gravity
clearly lost on HS, he had to partake in an assessment
carried out by a court appointed therapist; someone
allegedly trained in explaining the reasons why criminals
particapate in this sort of lurid behaviour. During these
sessions it had been established that HS had himself been
abused as a child, however, he refused to say by whom,
adding that the persons name was irrelevant, he just dealt
with it and moved on. It also transpired through the
questions of the examiner that throughout his life HS had
been a prolific predator of young children, mainly boys,
young adolescents of the impressionable age. In his twisted
mind he considered himself as just a father figure to most of
them and did not accept that he was responsible for a lot of
the endured mental torture by his victims.

While this type of phenomena was not a new condition
to be studied, it has been endemic down the ages, there
wasn't a lot known about the long term affects on individual
behaviour. There was a recognition however by
professionals-psychiatrists, psychologists that likened the
distress caused by any sort of sexual misconduct upon
minors similar to that of soldiers returning from war or
conflict situations.

Simon Sanders was not aware of such and struggled
through his adolescent years, his teenage years,
fundamentally growing up under the assumption that this
was part of lifes grand intention. It wasn't until after the
court case that he was afforded any help at all and made
aware of proper human behaviour. All of his self-doubting
and self loathing which was imposed on him, and in his
mind where paranoia plagued his every waking moment, he
came to realise also that this was not as he perceived how

everybody lived. It was soon discovered after one session with a psychiatrist that the young misunderstood Simon Sanders was afflicted with Post-Traumatic-Stress-Disorder with delayed onset. An affliction with an indeterminate lifespan...

Lightning Source UK Ltd.
Milton Keynes UK
25 January 2011

166308UK00001B/25/P